Towards a Better World

The path of maintenance for personal and social progress

Dr. Suresh Abhyankar

VISHWAKARMA
PUBLICATIONS VP©

Towards a Better World

The path of maintenance for personal and social progress

First Edition : January 2016
© Author

ISBN 978-81-927132-9-8

Published by:
Vishwakarma Publications
283, Budhwar Peth, Near City Post,
Pune - 411 002.
Phone No: 020 20261157
Email: info@vpindia.co.in
Website: www.vpindia.co.in

Cover Design
Abhishek Darekar
Vishwakarma Publications.

Typeset & Layout
Meghnad Deodhar
Vishwakarma Publications.

Index

Preface

Today we see that every person is unhappy about something or the other and is cribbing about the discomfort or the trouble he/she has faced because of 'this' or 'that'. Once upon a time, it was uneducated people who cribbed. It was because they did not understand the reasons behind their discomfort or inability to get things done. Today, the condition is quite different. Even highly-educated people crib about things and do not even try to understand the reasons behind their discomfort or in-ability to get something done.

As a management person when I started looking at the root cause of the many problems that most people face, I found that there are four basic reasons behind any discomfort or problem and they can be listed as below-

1. **Not following/maintaining the rules that are set up.**

2. **Not understanding the procedures.**

3. **Expecting more than what is humanly possible.**

4. **Expecting others to behave nicely while they themselves do not follow any norms.**

Now if we start looking at the reasons, point number one is applicable to both the parties (the service giver and service taker). But point number two, three and four are applicable to the person who begins complaining of someone else's role. No one talks about what he/she is expected to do but everyone talks about what others should do and what they are expected to do.

I found that the basic cause is that the maintenance of civic/society rules and regulations are utterly neglected by each and every one (barring a negligible few). If we start telling someone that he/she is wrong and should do their own home-work first and introspect before they start blaming others, no one likes it. It is not humanly possible for one or two people to try and educate all others about the maintenance of society and civic rules, so I felt that a book giving these tips would be the best option. If maximum number of people buy and read this book and propagate what is professed in it, to at least two or three people around them, one shall be able to see a complete change in society.

Here I would like to give an example of the city of Mumbai where in spite of having so much crowd in buses and local trains and on railway platforms, one hardly sees any fights between people. In Mumbai, all the people empathize with each other and know that all of them are RESPONSIBLE for the crowding and discomfort and so accept the reality and avoid fights.

Let all the people all over understand their own responsibility in the current situation of chaos and try to change themselves to make the situation bearable and comfortable for everyone.

Dr. Suresh Abhyankar

drsureshabhyankar@gmail.com

1. Personal Hygiene

When we talk about the maintenance of personal hygiene we must consider three distinct aspects which are -

- Clean body.
- Clean mind.
- Clean surroundings.

All the three points are inter-connected and cannot be separated from each other. Let us look at them individually and then connect them to each other.

Clean body: When we think of a clean body we must think in terms of a clean body externally and internally. External cleanliness is taught by our family elders, school teachers and friends. But nobody talks of internal cleanliness and so it is generally neglected. So let us first look at the internal cleanliness of the body.

Internal cleanliness of the body: When we talk about the internal cleanliness we need to talk about -

Ear : We have an external ear that is visible to everyone and we wash it when we take a bath or wash our face. But the internal ear or the tube leading to the diaphragm of the ear is always neglected by most of the people. Neglect of the internal ear leads to deafness in many people. Cleaning of the ear should be done properly by using soft ear buds and not by using a hard object, as it can damage the diaphragm and cause deafness and permanent damage to the internal ear.

·**Eyes:** Wash your eyes regularly. Use of protective goggles while travelling on the road or working in an industry is advisable so that no unwanted substance enters your eyes and harms them. You can do exercises for the eyes which will keep your vision clear.

Nose: Cleaning of the nose is a very important health aspect. The nose filters the air that is passing to the lungs. So if your nose is not functioning well, you can get attacked by various viruses and fall sick regularly. Cleaning of the nose should be a regular part of cleaning the face and body everyday. Ayurveda suggests cleaning of the nose by taking water from one nostril and taking it out from the other. But it is not easy and requires a lot of practice. The easiest way is to take water in your nostrils while taking a bath (if you are taking a shower it is easy) and throwing it out. This cleans your nose thoroughly and you can avoid common cold most of the time.

Doing Pranayama regularly helps avoid common

cold in more than 90% people.

Mouth: Oral health consists mainly of dental care, which depends on the following factors:

a. Regular brushing of teeth and massaging the gums.

b. Rinsing the mouth after you eat anything and ensuring that nothing that can decay is stuck in between your teeth.

c. If your teeth have gaps between them, use dental floss regularly.

d. Avoiding overeating which can lead to acidity (the acid that comes up in your mouth is harmful to your teeth.)

Various companies advertise various products for dental care and one can use them but we should remember that these products are effective only if you take care of your teeth in the way listed above. Even if you do not use any paste or powder for brushing your teeth and use your fingers for massaging the gums and rinse your mouth properly every time you eat something, your teeth can remain in good health. Companies use all manner of methods to lure people to use products without thinking of the deeper issues of whether they are brushing their teeth properly or rinsing their mouths after meals.

Many times, bad breath occurs due to improper digestion of food and improper sleep. Use of mouth fresheners cannot stop bad breath, if it is emanating from undigested food in your stomach. Late-night parties, heavy drinks, rich food and getting up late can lead to bad breath. Whenever you have late-night parties you should eat light food in a limited quantity to avoid bad breath the next day. Remember, it comes out of your stomach and not from your mouth.

Bad breath repels all the people around you.

Digestive system: The digestive system is the most neglected part of the body. Many people feel that if their stomach has come out it means that they are well-to-do and respectable. Actually when your stomach comes out, it is a sign of overeating and not being able to burn the calories you have consumed. Enlargement of stomach only happens when you overeat. You should only have food which is sufficient to take care of your body's needs. If you are not doing any physical activity, you should reduce your food intake and a person having high physical activity should eat smaller quantities of food, a number of times.

When you overeat, the following things happen -

a. If your digestive system is working well, your body converts the food into fat and it gets stored in thick layers around your waist.

b. If your digestive system is not so efficient, it leads to acidity, indigestion, headache, loose motions etc. and regular bouts of acidity which can lead to ulcers.

c. Overeating puts pressure on your stomach and its ability to secrete digestive fluids.

d. Overeating puts pressure on your liver and this can lead to permanent damage to your liver.

e. Overeating can lead to pressure on your pancreas and its inability to secrete enough insulin can lead to diabetes.

f. Overeating can lead to constipation which can lead to problems like piles.

g. Improper digestion is a major cause of bad breath.

h. Improper digestion is also a major cause of foul-smelling sweat and perspiration. No amount of body sprays can stop the bad smell of your body.

The best way to keep your body clean internally is to eat healthy food in the REQUIRED quantity and exercise regularly. More than 80% of grown-ups do not exercise regularly and fall prey to various kinds of body disorders. Most of these people claim that they do not have time for exercise. Ask the following questions and see what their answers will be -

1. What time do you wake up? 90% of the time they say around 5 am - 5.30 am - 6 am.

2. What do you do afterwards? Do morning chores and read the newspaper.

3. What do you read in the newspaper? Normally headlines, sports, advertisements for cinemas and drama etc.

4. What do you do afterwards? Take a bath and do Pooja, eat breakfast and get ready for office.

5. What time do you come back home? Usually

around 7 pm - 7.30 pm - sometimes by 8 pm.

6. What do you do afterwards? Watch TV.

7. What time you take dinner? Normally at 9 pm.

8. What time do you sleep? By 10.30 -11 pm

9. Why can't you spare 15-20 minutes in the morning or evening for exercise? Where is the time in such a busy schedule? There is no space in my house to exercise.

10. Why don't you take a walk after dinner which is also a good exercise?

I walk a lot during the day, like I walk up to the bus stop. 'No time' is clearly an excuse for not exercising. One can very well see that almost all the people have enough time to exercise but the willingness to do so is absent. Every time you meet them, they have gained weight and are progressing from fat to obese. As a marketing person, I have travelled all over the country and outside and have seen many ambitious people exercising even in the smallest hotel rooms or in the corridors, if gyms are not available. They know that if they want to progress in their career path, they must remain fit, healthy and smart. If marketing people who move from one location to the other every second day and who have no fixed time for food and sleep (buses, trains and airlines decide their time of sleep and waking up) can find time to exercise, all other people should be able to exercise. Software companies have arrangements for all their employees to exercise in their in-house gyms but hardly anyone uses them and most of the employees are obese. Eating cheese and junk food and not doing exercise leads to obesity and ill health.

Exercise and internal cleanliness of the body:

Exercise helps all the internal and external organs function properly and its benefits can be easily listed as follows -

- Exercise makes your body supple and gives it good form.

- It builds your muscles and increases their strength.

- It builds your stamina.

- It helps in improving the blood circulation and also the oxygen supply to all parts and organs of the body.

- It leads to increased sweating and helps remove toxic substances from your body through sweat.

- It helps burn accumulated body fats, improves the functioning of the liver and kidney and helps to remove toxins from your body effectively.

- It helps the body to digest food effectively and gives you the required strength.

- It can help you remain healthy and avoid catching illness (improves the immune system).

- It keeps your body fresh and energetic for a longer time.

Regular exercise does not mean daily exercise but one can have a schedule of two/three/four days a week for exercising. However, it should be followed without fail. If one is unable to have a fixed timing for exercising, he/she can do so any time of the day/night. Many of our actors like Salman Khan, Aamir Khan are known to exercise even at midnight to keep fit and they are successful because of their appearance.

When we say exercise, it can be of any form and one can choose from any of the following forms -

- Jogging
- Running
- Walking
- Aerobics
- Treadmill
- Exer-cycle
- Weight training
- Yoga
- Various indoor and outdoor games (not cards and chess or carom)

External cleaning of the body: Taking a bath daily is very important for keeping your body clean and healthy. In India, the non-availability of enclosed toilets and bathrooms prevents people from cleaning their anus and genitals properly, leading to many diseases of these parts and the urinary tract. Use of soap is a must as it helps remove all the dirt from your body effectively. In Arabian countries, the practice of circumcision of genitals was started in view of the non-availability of water to clean that part. Today there are many elderly men who are advised to get circumcised to prevent urinary tract infections. To keep the body clean, every household must have enclosed toilets and bathrooms with running water.

Washing hair daily is advisable but if you are maintaining long hair then whenever you take a head bath, use of Shampoo/shikakai is a must to ensure that your hair and scalp are properly cleaned of all the dust and oil.

One should take a bath twice a day in a tropical country like India to ensure that the body is cleaned properly. Lot of dust particles stick to your body due to the sweating of the body and it should be washed properly so that the skin pores remain clean and open to sweat properly. One can take bath once a day during winters.

Washing hands as many times as possible is advisable and you should wash your legs at least twice a day. Washing the face is also a must at least twice a day using soap as facial skin is very vulnerable to an attack of germs.

Many people take a bath with their clothes on due to the non-availability of a closed bathroom. So these people are in a hurry to finish their bath and are shy of cleaning their covered parts properly, especially their genitals. There are plenty of cases of urinary tract infection only because these parts are not cleaned regularly and properly. One should not feel shy of cleaning these parts as it can lead to serious health problems of a permanent nature.

Maintaining body hygiene helps keep your body fit and

healthy. It is very easy to do so and one should be alert about it. I am not telling anyone to miss out on the enjoyments of life but one cannot keep enjoying life without taking care of one's body. Unless your body is healthy there is no enjoyment. If you overeat on a particular day, you should avoid/reduce your next meal. If you had a long day and less sleep, try to catch up on your sleep whenever possible and give your body the required rest.

Do not overdo anything, as excess of everything is harmful to your body. Maintain health and hygiene for a longer life.

Personality & Personal hygiene

Personality is connected to personal hygiene to a great extent. People tend to relate personality to their grooming (going to beauty parlours - both men and women, and wearing expensive clothes of foreign labels). In our school days we used to have a lesson where a rich man's son wearing expensive clothes is weak with decayed teeth and a middle class boy has healthy habits and simple washed clothes. The middle class boy with healthy habits is chosen as a student with good personality. I think we have stopped teaching these kinds of lessons.

Anyone with a good physique (a result of healthy and hygienic habits) looks smarter and attractive if he is wearing clean and neat clothes. There is no need to wear clothes with foreign labels (it is a waste of foreign exchange in royalties as the clothes are manufactured in

India only).

Do not wear trendy clothes if they do not suit your physique. In India we can still afford to get our clothes tailor-made, and these clothes look smarter. But we may be influenced by fashion to wear readymade clothes that are ill-fitting and uncomfortable. In fact, sometimes such trendy clothes may even be making us look ugly. Let us make the effort to wear well-fitting and smart clothes.

Points to Ponder

1. Brush your teeth at least once a day.

2. Take bath every day. Ensure that you clean your genitals properly while taking bath.

3. Wash your face at least twice a day.

4. Wash your hands and legs every time you go out of the house and come back.

5. Exercise every day no matter what your age is; do not overdo it. You should sweat but not get tired.

6. Take proper sleep of 6-8 hours (as per your age).

7. Take healthy food (avoid junk food), do not over-eat or remain on an empty stomach.

8. Eat lots of salads and also include sprouts.

9. Eat leafy vegetables at least once a week.

10. Eat all the seasonal fruits.

2. Social Sanitation and Hygiene

We looked at personal hygiene in the earlier chapter, but the major problem is the maintenance of social hygiene. Let us look at various important points where most of the people neglect the maintenance of social hygiene.

Throwing dirt/litter/solid waste/garbage outside: Many people are proud of their cleanliness and wash and clean their houses twice or thrice a day. But after cleaning their house of all the dirt/litter/solid waste, they throw it out of their house, thus making the surroundings dirty. Are they doing it for the purpose of comparing the cleanliness of their house with their surroundings? If yes, they should know that more number of people pass the surrounding of their houses than come inside to see their house. Such people may be wondering how these people manage to stay in such a dirty place! Thus, when we contribute to the dirt outside our homes, we are always harming ourselves, even though we keep the inside of our houses sparkling clean.

Some people do better than the above-mentioned people and along with their houses, clean a portion of their surroundings and push all the garbage

/dirt/litter/solid waste outside their own demarcated area. Now these people are a little aware of the cleanliness of their surroundings but are lazy enough to not collect all the dirt together and give it to the municipal van that comes to collect the dirt from every house and dump it in the dumping ground. If they take this little extra effort they will be saved more efforts next time as most of the time, the dirt and foliage of the trees is blown back into their houses and surroundings by the wind.

Civic authorities ask people to segregate solid waste into wet (bio-degradable) and dry (non-biodegradable) solid waste while handing it over. It is important for solid waste to be segregated and given separately to reduce the efforts of the civic authorities in managing the solid waste accumulating from the cities and towns. Some of the civic authorities in big cities have introduced fines on citizens for not segregating the solid waste, but all to no effect.

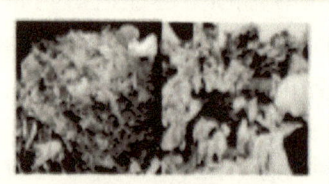

Non-Segregation of
Bio-degradable
Waste Fine - Rs. 100/-

Throwing things from the window: In most of the housing societies and apartments dedicated sweeper is appointed who collects the solid waste from each house and sweeps the staircases and surroundings. In turn, the sweeper gives the collected wasted to the municipal van collecting solid waste. This is done once in a day, mostly during the morning hours. But there are many people, especially house–wives who keep throwing things out from their kitchen and other windows. When they are caught throwing things, they say, "It's a mistake. I only did it today. What has happened to me today? May be the headache I am having is making me do such things." I think these house-wives have a severe headache every day and keep throwing things out of the windows regularly. If we don't catch them red-handed and complain about things coming out of their windows, they blame their children and many times even guests coming to their houses occasionally.

There are many places in Europe where the solid waste from residential areas is collected once a week and not daily, but these people store the solid waste properly till it is collected by the civic authorities. In a tropical country like India, the storage of solid waste is not possible for more than a day or two but it is the responsibility of each and every person to keep his/her surroundings clean.

A peculiar thing is observed in many housing complexes where the apartment houses are managed by their own members and people staying in row houses and bungalows manage their own affairs. In such cases it is found that instead of appointing a sweeper to collect the solid waste (the sweeper charges more money from these owners as they expect him to collect the solid waste and also sweep their individual surroundings) the owners of row houses and bungalows prefer to throw it in the open space of the housing complex early in the morning or late in the evenings. These people should understand that the cost of maintenance is definitely going to be higher for individual houses than for apartment owners and they should either be willing to take that additional burden or should stay in apartment houses. One cannot have one's cake and eat it too!

Why can't people accept unpalatable facts about themselves? Accepting that we have bad habits and doing penance for the same can cure anyone's bad habits. In India, we have the greatest example of 'Valya Koli' accepting his mistakes, doing penance and becoming the greatest poet who wrote the Ramayana.

It is the responsibility of every person to maintain social hygiene and many civic authorities are forced to introduce fines for such offences.

1. **Throwing litter on the road and open spaces:** Throwing litter on the road is a common habit of 90% of Indians. The reason, many give is, "Where do we throw it otherwise?" There are no dustbins to be seen anywhere. It is true to a large extent as in most of the public spaces, there is no facility to throw litter, but that does not mean that people should throw it anywhere. The maximum litter which is thrown on the roads is by the people who eat Gutkha and smoke cigarettes/bidis. More than 30% of the Indian population is in the habit of eating Gutkha and that too on an average, 10 packets a day. This alone creates litter of 400 crore Gutkha packets on the road. Can these people not keep the empty Gutkha packets in their pockets till such time that they see a

litter box somewhere? No civic body can make arrangements to have litter boxes at every corner of every road. Maintaining them would require a lot of money which people are not willing to pay as tax.

Theft of these boxes by rag pickers is another problem as selling them to any 'kabadi' earns them their daily wage in one shot.

Another group that litters the roads is the street vendors selling fruits, vegetables and snacks like

bhel and pani-puri. These people clean the fruits and vegetables and throw the litter on the roads. Snack-sellers wash the dishes on the roads and also throw the litter on the road. Punishing all the gutkha-eaters is physically not possible considering their sheer numbers but punishing the vegetable fruit sellers and the snack sellers is easy. Civic authorities take bribes from these people and let them litter the streets. Actually speaking, snacks are prepared in unhygienic conditions and that too on the road, so both are cognizable offences and liable for severe punishment. Actually the severity of the punishment only raises the amount of bribe and all the offenders are allowed to go scot-free and that is how many of the poorly paid civic staff are found to be have big properties and bank balances.

Like in other countries (not only western but also in

the far eastern countries which are much cleaner than India) the road-side food vendors must be asked to serve food in non-reusable recyclable/bio-degradable containers. The people who purchase these items can pay for the packaging. It should be the responsibility of the food-seller to collect all the used

containers and dump them at the solid waste collection centres. This will ensure public hygiene as well as sanitation.

2. **Spitting on the road and open spaces:** There are two reasons why people spit on the roads and in open spaces

   • The surroundings are dusty and smelly: In this case the person who is spitting cannot be blamed as he/she is spitting out of nauseating conditions.

   • Spitting out of habit: As mentioned earlier, more than 30% people have a habit of eating Gutkha, chewing tobacco or betel leaves along with tobacco. All these people are compulsive spitters. Spitting has become so natural to them that they do not realise that they are spitting. If they spit on some passerby they say, "It is only tobacco and not vomit,". As if spitting tobacco is less dirty than vomiting.

   Once I was standing at the arrival point of an airport and saw a group of Indians coming out after a visit to Singapore. They asked their friends and family members, "Have you brought my paan?" After eating the paan they spat merrily and said, "Since the last eight days I have had no paan; now I feel at home. The pleasure in spitting the paan is something only we can understand. It is not that you don't get paan in Singapore, but spitting in Singapore attracts a hefty fine and repetition of the offence can lead to imprisonment."

Actually, spitting in public spaces is the biggest cause of spreading Tuberculosis (TB) in India. TB, with 2.3 million new cases annually is causing 3,20,000 deaths every year. In India, an estimated 400 million people, a number larger than the entire population of the USA, are infected with the TB bacillus, but are asymptomatic though at risk of developing active TB. All this can be avoided only if people decide not to spit in public places.

3. **Using open spaces as urinals and toilets:** Open defecation is a social disease in India. Even after passing a regulation that people not having toilets at home cannot contest elections even for Panchayat Raj, people do not build toilets at home. Many people, even after having a proper toilet prefer to go out and defecate in an open space and say, "Dam ghutata hain toilet mein (I become breathless in the toilet)."

Openly defecating in rural India can be blamed on non-availability of water easily to most households. Toilets require a huge quantity of water to flush (approximately 50 litres in Indian toilets and 100 litres in English/commode toilets per family of 4-5 persons) and that would be an additional burden on the women of the house who fetch water approximately 4-5 kms away from their houses. Government authorities have offered subsidies to build toilets (but it is said that a part of it goes into the pockets of Government officials and local leaders) and a lot of propaganda was done to emphasize the importance of toilets, but they have done nothing to ensure availability of water to rural people nearer to their houses easily. Fifty percent of the rural population opts for open defecation due to the scarcity of water. Government authorities will succeed in stopping

open defecation only when water scarcity is eradicated from rural India.

Urban population residing in slums that does not face water scarcity opts for open defecation, for want of common toilets. Civic authorities build common toilets but in many places, they are immediately taken over by anti-social elements for running their operations of selling drugs, bootlegging or gambling. No one dares to complain against them and even Government authorities, including police do not take action against them. So civic authorities should do the following to stop open defecation in urban areas:

- Do not allow slums to develop.
- Provide enough common toilets with running water in slums.
- Ensure that anti-social elements do not take over these common toilets for their nefarious activities.

4. **Taking dogs out for a walk and allowing the dog to excrete on roads and footpaths:** Many people have dogs as pets and take the dogs out in the morning and evening for walks. They think that all people love dogs but are unable to purchase a pedigree dog for themselves. Many of them have adopted a street dog and do not understand the difference between a scoundrel and a pedigree dog. These dogs defecate on the roads and footpaths (they are animals) and their owners (supposed to be civilized human beings) are not at all bothered about the nuisance they are creating to other citizens. They think laws are only applicable to humans and not to the dogs. *I have a feeling that while walking a dog in the open, if the owner is compelled to carry a spatula and a bag, more than half the proud owners of the dogs will stop having a pet dog.* In India, there are no proper laws on pets. The people owning pets may love their pets (seems doubtful, as many times they are found going out of station and locking their pets in the house without arranging for any care. The pet creates so much noise and nuisance for the entire neighbourhood that sometimes the neighbours are

forced to call the police) but they should take care that the pets are not creating any nuisance to the other citizens, especially the neighbours. It has been found that -

- People do not register their pets as they do not want to pay civic tax on pets.

- People do not vaccinate their pets.

- People do not give anti-rabies shots to their dogs.

- People abandon their pets while changing houses.

- They do not leash their dogs while walking.

- When stray dogs attack the pet dog, the owners start hitting stray dogs. If you love dogs you should not hit strays as they are also dogs.

- If the dogs defecate on roads and footpaths or open spaces in societies it is the owners' responsibility to clean it. The dog owners never do it.

While we are talking on dogs we must understand the problems that are created by stray dogs. Statistics say that around 40% deaths due to rabies worldwide are happening in India (55,000 worldwide, India-approx. 35,000) and most of them are due to dog bites. We are not against animals. While humans are not allowed to kill animals, we should not allow animals (dogs) to kill humans. All life is precious, but we should take care to create such conditions wherein all can live with security. Animal welfare organizations emphasize controlling the population of stray dogs through ABC (animal birth control), and civic authorities must ensure this programme is vigorously carried out. Prevention is better than killing

of stray animals, which brings municipal corporations into controversy.

Stray dog menace also leads to road accidents, which are not reported. Death due to rabies also goes under death by road accident. If we add road accident deaths due to stray dogs, the toll will cross 50,000 deaths.

5. **Polluting the rivers:** River pollution has reached such a level that we have rivers only in the rainy season and sewerage gutters for the rest of the year. Rajiv Gandhi, as Prime Minister of India talked about cleaning the Ganga and other rivers and making them pollution-free in late 1980s but it has remained a pipe dream.

   Civic bodies still allow the sewerage to flow into rivers without treating it.

   • Construction contractors still throw debris in the rivers.

   • People throw all their unwanted things on the river banks.

- Vehicles are washed in the rivers.

- Animals are washed in the rivers.

- Ganesh/Durga idols are immersed in the rivers.

- Dead bodies of humans and animals are thrown in the rivers without cremating them.

- Ashes of people are immersed in rivers.

- The eateries and shops along the river banks throw all their waste materials in the rivers.

- Chemical factories dump their hazardous materials in the rivers.

- Sugar factories/tanneries release their waste into the rivers without treating it.

I am yet to understand the thinking behind depositing the nirmalya (flowers offered to God and removed the next day) in the gutters called rivers in all the cities in India. The old tradition had a value system when the rivers were clean and the used flowers would get deposited on the banks of rivers and the flowering plants would come up on the river banks, With the current state of the rivers (gutters), it adds on to the pollution of the river because the flowers immediately start rotting and don't germinate into flowering plants. It is better to dump the nirmalya in potted plants or a compost pit or dry and burn it rather than throwing it in the polluted rivers.

How do we keep the rivers clean and un-polluted? India, with the highest amount of fresh water availability wastes fresh water on washing cars;

gardening etc. while it has water scarcity in many areas. Cities like Chennai are thinking about desalination of sea water but the Adyar river is always a sewerage canal throughout the year, so why not take steps to make it pollution-free?

6. **Throwing things in gutters:** Many people consider gutters and drains as dustbins and throw anything and everything in gutters (open gutters and drains are common in almost all cities/towns and villages). These drains and gutters are cleaned every year before the monsoon so that they do not choke and flood the adjoining areas. This is a big drain and financial burden on the civic authorities. Most of the time, the flood-affected people are ones who throw things in the open gutters and drains throughout the year. The civic authorities should declare that the drains will not be cleaned if the people staying in the area do not stop throwing things in the gutters and open drains and let them suffer one year for their misdeeds. But the elected representatives want to take credit for cleaning the drains and make money in commissions from it every year.

7. **Throwing bio-medical waste:** Medical doctors are supposed to take care of the health of the people in the society but if they are themselves involved in creating conditions that help spread contagious diseases, then their sincerity in protecting people comes under a cloud of suspicion and people start

thinking that they are helping the spread of diseases to improve their business.

That the civic authorities are not providing the facility to throw and burn bio-medical waste cannot be an excuse, as most of the clinics and nursing homes are not even registered with the civic authorities and do not pay the required tax for civic authorities to provide such services to them. The reason given for not registering is that there are strict rules for registration (where one can open a clinic/nursing home and what kind of minimum infrastructure they should have). By not registering and saving on taxes, are these people offering the services at affordable rates to their patients? The answer is a big NO. Actually these people are found to be charging more fees than even big and reputed hospitals and have lesser facilities and infrastructure.

8. **Throwing rubble (waste building materials) anywhere:** With the citizens' incomes going up with high salaries in many private organizations and high rates of corruption, in Government and Semi-Government staff, renovations of the residences every second year has become a norm. The rubble created by this is thrown in any corner of the city/town/village creating serious problems to the general cleanliness of the society. The person who gets the renovation done blames the contractor but is it not the joint responsibility of the contractor and the person getting the renovation done to ensure that the

rubble is thrown in a proper dumping ground provided by the civic authorities?

It is the responsibility of the civic authorities that they should create a facility to collect the rubble and throw it in a proper dumping ground for a fee payable by the renovator/contractor.

Points to ponder

1. Do not throw garbage/litter out of your house. Give it to the sweeper/garbage collector.

2. Do not throw garbage/litter on the streets or open spaces. Throw it in garbage bins kept for this purpose.

3. If you are running a food stall on the road, ensure that both your customers and you do not throw remnants and waste on the road, but throw it in the garbage bins nearby.

4. Do not urinate /defecate in the open. Instead, use toilets.

5. The Government should try and introduce waterless (chemical) toilets all over India which will eliminate the necessity of water and which will be acceptable to all.

6. If you are having pets, ensure that they do not defecate in the open and make streets/open spaces dirty. Carry a spatula and broom and collect the pet's shit in a bag and throw it in the garbage bins nearby.

7. Do not throw anything in rivers and pollute them.

8. Do not throw anything in open gutters and drains

Non-Segregation of
Bio-Medical
Waste Fine - Rs. 20.000/-

Urinating Fine - Rs. 200/-

Litter by Pet Fine - Rs. 500/-

Defecating Fine - Rs. 100/-

(nallas), as they get choked, creating problems for others.

9. Do not throw rubble just anywhere but in a place allocated for it by the civic authorities.

10. If you are running a clinic/nursing home, ensure that you destroy bio-chemical waste properly.

11. Prevention is better than cure, so do not allow your surroundings to get dirty and keep them clean.

12. Civic authorities should ensure that people keep the place clean by being vigilant and imposing fine on miscreants.

13. Civic authorities should ensure enough piped water supply and availability of toilets, so that people can use them (It is not necessary that they should be free of charge).

14. Civic authorities should ensure there are no stray dogs troubling citizens.

15. Civic authorities responsible for cleanliness should be penalized heavily for neglecting their job responsibilities. No leniency should be shown towards such people.

3. Personal Vehicles

Each and every person has a desire to own a personal vehicle, whether a cycle, scooter/motorcycle or a car. In Pune, Bengaluru, Nagpur and most of the cities in India except Mumbai, it is most important to have one`s own vehicle if you need to travel across the city ON TIME. This is so because of the inadequate and improperly planned public transport service provided by most of the cities. People buy two wheelers and four wheelers and use them regularly. But most people think that servicing is required only when the vehicle is new and so, after the three free servicing sessions do not bother to get their vehicles serviced. But they do not know that servicing must be done regularly for the maintenance of the vehicles and for them to remain in good shape.

Two Wheelers:

While travelling on the road, sometimes we see two wheelers being pushed by the owners and in Pune we also see a friend pushing the two-wheeler by pushing it with one leg and driving his own vehicle. The reasons are

1. No petrol in the vehicle.

2. The vehicle has stopped automatically and is not starting.

Situation 1. These people are looking for the nearest petrol pump or a mechanic. The people who are searching for petrol pumps invariably crib about the men at the petrol pump who do not giving petrol in a bottle, as they need to go up to the petrol pump and fetch the petrol to start the vehicle.

Is it wrong on the part of the men at the petrol pump? No, definitely not, because with the fear of a terrorist attack looming large everywhere, how will anyone know who is a possible terrorist and who is not. In such a case it is advisable to refuse issuing petrol in any container other than in the petrol tank of a vehicle. (A terrorist can take it out from there too, but it is not very easy. A precaution is always the best solution). But we are cribbers by habit and whenever we are in trouble we expect others to break the rules and help us. Why? Because we feel that these people are breaking the rules regularly and only when we approach them then they show us the rule book.

Why do we not check the petrol level every day? Why do we run our two wheelers on the reserve position of the petrol cock? "Because this is a free country and we will behave the way we want to."

Situation 2. Ask these people when was the last time they had serviced their vehicle. Nine out of ten times the answer is - two wheelers do not require servicing after the first three free servicing sessions.

Ask them when was the last time they cleaned their vehicles? Seven out of ten times, the answer is at the time of Dassera i.e. once in a year.

Ask then, when was the spark plug cleaned? The answer mostly is, "The last time the vehicle stopped and the mechanic changed the old one. After that I have not cleaned it any time."

If this is the condition of the transmission system what is the condition of say

1. Breaks and break liners.

2. Carburetors.

3. Rear view mirrors.

4. Indicator lights.

5. Horn.

6. Head light.

7. Break light.

How many times do we blame the other person for the accidents that occur because of our own ill-maintained vehicle?

It has been found that 90% of the two wheelers do not have rear view mirrors and these two wheeler riders blatantly zoom at very high speed on the road, cutting lanes and moving between the small gaps in between the four wheelers/trucks, cutting corners of these vehicles. When there is an accident, the four wheeler/truck drivers are blamed for high speed when in reality, the two wheeler driver is at fault. Two wheelers should have separate lanes on roads and should be banned on highways,　just as they are not allowed on expressways.

Four Wheelers:

While travelling we also see motor cars being pushed aside and the reasons are again

1. No petrol in the vehicle.

2. Vehicle stopped automatically and is not starting.

Situation 3. These people will invariably go to the nearest petrol pump and demand petrol in a can/bottle and when refused, will start fighting with the men at the petrol pump. The argument these times are -

a. Can't you see that we are respectable people and not terrorists?

b. Take double the amount but give me petrol.

c. Send your man with me up to my car, and I will give him the auto fare back along with a good tip.

d. I will call the authorities and ensure that your petrol pump is closed down for–ever.

e. Why are you telling me the rules? As if you never break them!

And many more, but the best one, "Please give us petrol only this once, there are women and small children in the car.... Please be human and help me."

Why don't we check fuel every day? There is no answer to this.

Situation 4. Ask these people when was the last time they serviced their vehicle? 'Last year after monsoon' is the most likely answer. The next question you ask is, "How many kilometers do you travel every month?" 30-50 OR 80-100 kms every day is the answer. A motor car requires servicing after every 3000 to 5000 kms run, so by that standard, cars should be serviced every two or three months to avoid breakdowns on the road.

Battery condition is another reason for cars stopping. It is found that the service stations do not ever check the battery unless you tell them specifically to do so. One should check the battery fluid every two to three months if the battery is not the maintenance-free type. Replace the battery after its life is over.

Most of the people do not check the following regularly if their vehicle is not serviced on time

1. Air pressure in tyres.

2. Break oil.

3. Engine oil.

4. Coolant level.

5. Water in the wiper tank.

If you want to use the vehicle for any reason, be it necessity or esteem (show-off) you must maintain it properly. Remember you are not the only person who gets troubled by your vehicle breakdown but you hold up and disturb the entire road traffic.

Situation 5: I was travelling with my friend and I found that the vehicle was rattling. I said that there was some problem with the vehicle but my friend said that the problem was not with the vehicle but with the road. The road had many craters and he was finding it difficult to avoid them. I insisted that we check the tyres, but my friend said that he had changed the tyres the day before for this trip. So there was no question of having a flat tyre. Because I was insistent, he stopped and checked and found that one tyre had gone flat and when we checked the tube, it needed to be replaced because it was completely shattered.

My friend who owns and drives a car since the last 20 years could not understand the situation and had a feeling that flat tyres are only possible when they are worn out. My friend is not an isolated person as there are many such drivers/car owners and this ignorance can lead to losing control over the vehicle and an accident can happen. One should be more careful and sensitive to the movement of the car. Actually, when there is a flat tyre, there is an additional pressure on the steering wheel and the car pulls on the side of the flat tyre.

Situation 6: I was travelling with my neighbours to an advocate's office, when the neighbour who was driving us said, "Mr. Abhyankar, you have been driving a car for many years, can you tell me why my car shows a high temperature immediately after starting and remains at a high level?"

I asked him, "Have you checked the radiator and the coolant?"

He said, "Yes."

I asked, "Have you checked the engine oil?"

He asked, "What is that?"

I asked him to stop at the nearest petrol pump and fill one litre engine oil. When we started the car, it showed normal temperature.

Situation 7: My client reported that his car had suddenly stopped midway and he would be delayed for the meeting. When he came I asked him, "What was the problem?" He said that there was no fluid in the battery even when the car had been serviced two days ago. I told him that when the mechanics do the servicing they do not check the battery unless you tell them to, so either he should start using service-free battery or check the fluid regularly himself.

Actually speaking, one is not required to be an expert or experienced for all this. When you purchase the vehicle, there is always a handbook of maintenance given to the purchaser which explains all these situations. But the question is how many of us read these instructions? I would ask, how many of us keep the manual properly?

Points to Ponder:

1. Keep your vehicle clean and in good running condition to avoid problems on the road while driving.
2. Servicing the vehicle after using it for 1000-3000 kms keeps it in good running condition and also saves fuel.
3. Check fuel level/lights the first thing everyday.
4. Check tyre pressure regularly.
5. For batteries requiring servicing, check the water level regularly.
6. Check brake/engine oil levels regularly.
7. Check the coolant and water (for wipers) level regularly.
8. Ensure PUC checks are done properly and emission levels are at the permissible levels.
9. In case of accidents due to poor servicing and bad condition of the vehicles, the owners should not get compensation and should be penalized for causing harm to other people.
10. Ensure that the vehicle has rear view mirrors in place.
11. Wear helmets while riding two wheelers (both the riders).
12. Do not use bright headlights in the city, as it affects the drivers of the incoming vehicles.

◆◆◆◆

4. Following Road Safety Rules

Most people do not know what the road safety rules are, as most of them know them as traffic rules. Change the nomenclature and your attitude towards these rules changes to the positive side, as everyone is concerned about the safety of individuals on the road.

When we want to take a driving license, we want to have it without any hassles, so we search for an agent who will ensure that we are not required to go through the test. Why? "Because the RTO authorities ask me the traffic rules and the meanings of the road signs, and I do not know them." Do we ever think why it is important to know the rules and the meaning of the road signs?

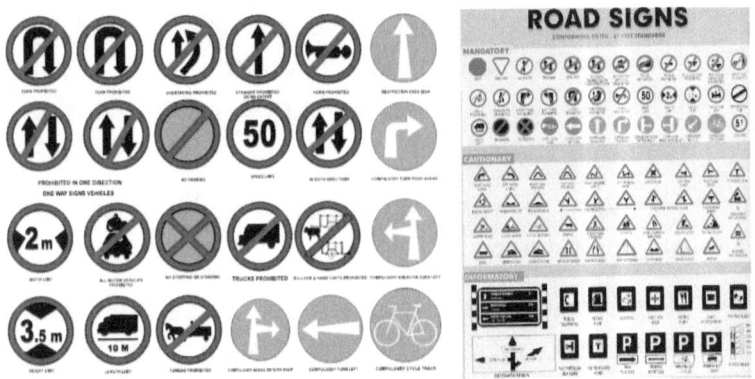

Fig. 4.1 Road Safety Signs

Look at the road signs given above as all these signs are for your own safety for avoiding accidents. Don't ever think that in an accident, the other person will get injured and you will be spared. So do not take the easy way out even if you fail the test once or twice, ensure that you learn all the rules properly and then start using the vehicles. It is good for both, your safety and the safety of the public at large.

You should be proud of actually attempting and passing the RTO test rather than being proud of getting your license without attempting the test (by bribing and then cribbing about corruption in public life). Be proud of following rules rather than not following/breaking rules.

Attitude Changes Required:

1. These rules have been devised for my safety and the safety of other people using the roads.

2. Accidents can happen to anyone; even I can be involved in them. Let us prevent accidents by following road safety rules.

3. Accidents can happen by the mistake of one person. The person making a mistake need not be you, but you can always prevent it by being cautious.

4. The other person is not at fault every time; you can also be at fault.

5. When you are a pedestrian you curse the vehicle drivers. Do not make pedestrians curse you. Follow road safety rules.

6. Pedestrian crossing signals are meant for safely crossing roads and not for smart people to move ahead of fools who are waiting for the signal to turn green!

7. A person honking is not always honking for you to shift, but may-be for some other fool who is not following the rules. Do not increase your speed, he/she may be asking for side clearance.

8. Do not get offended if someone overtakes you from the wrong/left side. It is possible that you are not giving him side on the right or you are travelling very slowly in the right lane.

9. Give a signal when you are turning or even changing lanes, as others cannot read your mind.

10. Do not cut corners while taking a right turn as you cannot see the oncoming vehicles from the right (maximum accidents take place due to this).

11. You are not the only intelligent person on earth. Others also can have knowledge and intelligence.

12. You do not own the road; it is for everyone to use, so do not block all the lanes and allow others to use the remaining road (this holds true particularly for two wheeler riders, as they ride in the centre of the road leaving no place for others).

Once the attitude changes, life will become a lot easier for everyone. Think of an average person who travels for at least half an hour towards his/her workplace and half an hour back home every day. In that half hour he/she is tense about possible accidents and unruly behaviour of co-travellers on the road. This tension can lead to the preparation of defence and possible offence. When I came to Pune, one of my cousins told me, "Never admit that you are wrong because that can lead to trouble. In Pune, the person who is shouting loudly and trying to prove himself/herself right is mostly wrong. In Mumbai, I had this habit of saying sorry even though I was not in the wrong, while travelling in crowded railways. Actually, if we decide not to make a mistake and accept our fault and say sorry, life becomes a lot more easy. Once upon a time there used to be a 'SOUJANYA SAPTAH' every year. I do not know why it was stopped but it really shows you that saying sorry is the best way to succeed in social life.

Look at the following situations where breaking the rule is of no benefit.

Situation 1: Travelling on the Wrong Side of the Road.

The road dividers are ideally placed with a cut every 50 metres, so that anyone who wants to be on the other side has to travel a maximum of 50 metres in the other direction, cross the divider and retrace his way towards where he actually wants to go. Only on very busy roads the 'U' turns may not be allowed immediately and you have to travel more than 50 metres before you take a 'U' turn On busy roads, people travelling on the wrong track are less. Now what are the reasons or benefits you get by travelling on the wrong track? I don't know if there are any more than these listed below:

- You save time.

- You save fuel.

- You satisfy your EGO.

- You do not know it is illegal.

Do you really save time? The answer is NO. Because you are travelling on the wrong side, you have to drive cautiously (unless you are a Mawali/goon who does not care) spending more time and getting abused by people.

Do you save fuel? Again the answer is the same - NO. You travel slower than the economic speed of 40 kmph and end up spending more fuel or saving a negligible amount of less than a rupee (with fuel efficiency of 50km/l for two wheelers and 12 km/l for car). Do you want to risk your life and are you willing to take abuses from the public for such a small amount?

You satisfy your EGO. Yes, you definitely satisfy your EGO but at what cost? Are you sure that when you break the law you get importance?

You do not know it is illegal. In that case you are not eligible to get a driving license.

Situation 2: Travelling in NO ENTRY

The benefits and reasons of travelling in the NO ENTRY zone are the same as listed above for travelling in the wrong direction.

- You save time.

- You save fuel.

- You satisfy your EGO.

- You do not know it is illegal.

- Everyone does it, so what is the big deal if I also do so?

Do you really save time? The answer many times is YES, but are we not reducing the speed of the traffic and wasting the time of others? Are you so selfish that you only care about your time? Are you so important a person? And what is the reason behind the saving of your time? Are you going for some work of national importance? Or are you a trying to save the life of people who are in danger, and would it affect them if you do not reach in time?

Some people habitually travel in the NO ENTRY zone to save time. Why can't they start in time, to reach in time by following the rules?

Do you save fuel? Again the answer in many cases is YES, but living in a society has its benefits and drawbacks. You must forego a little to get the larger benefits in life. It is possible that by travelling in the NO ENTRY zone, you may be involved in a fatal accident and you may be the one to lose life. Anything is possible.

You satisfy your EGO. Yes, you definitely satisfy your EGO but at what cost? Are you sure that when you break the law, you get importance?

You do not know it is illegal. In such a case you are not eligible to get a driving license.

Everyone does it so I am also doing it. This is the worst attitude, but unfortunately this is true for many. In a city like Pune, I also see very old people breaking traffic rules (normally common for youngsters) and having the same attitude.

Situation 3: Travelling with Full Light in the City

In a city or town with street lighting, vehicles are expected to travel with parking lights only (e.g. Mumbai). But I see many people blazing full lights even on roads that are over-illuminated due to street lights plus the shop lights. Some vehicles are fitted with sodium lights and travel with full lights. Actually, full lights are to be used only on highways and for giving signals to upcoming vehicles.

What must be reason behind this?

The answer can be

- We do not know that lights can be dimmed.
- Others are using full lights so we also use full lights.

Are they rational reasons? No, but they are true and many people will vouch for the same.

Situation 4: Travelling with the Entire Family on a Two Wheeler (husband, wife and two/three or more children).

Most of the time I find people travelling with the entire family on a two wheeler and going at very high speeds and breaking traffic rules. People are forced to give side to these reckless drivers out of pity and care for the small children.Talk to these people and they are proud of doing so and saving money being spent on autos and taxis, but at what cost? A small mistake and one can lose one's entire family. Is saving money so important? If you want to save money, reduce your outings, travel on Sundays as there is lots of time to spare and use public transport. These people should be fined heavily or should be jailed to stop them from repeating the same.

Situation 5: Autos/Vans Ferrying School Children.

The drivers of autos/vans that carry school children feel that no road safety rules are applicable to them, so they do the following -

- Carry more number of children than they are authorized to carry.
- Have no safety precautions fitted to their vehicles.
- Travel at high speed.
- Break the RED signals.
- Travel on the wrong side.
- Travel through NO ENTRY.
- Talk to children while driving.
- Use mobiles while driving.

I do not understand why they are allowed to do so? I even do not understand why parents do not object to the number of children being ferried?

This autos/van drivers take charges for all the twelve months (some ask for bonus also) and that too at very high rates. If two or three parents pool and take the responsibility to take their children turn by turn, they may actually end up saving money. I can understand the plight of working parents but the children of housewives who do not want to take the trouble and risk the life of the child, is a point to ponder and wonder.

Situation 6: Turning on Roads.

People taking turns without giving signals is becoming very common. No one can dream that you intend to take a right or left turn, and the vehicle behind you can lose control and there can be an accident just because you have not given the signal. I have seen people say that they stay there and that they take that turn everyday. OK, so you know that you take a turn here every day, but why do you expect others to know about it? Everyday the same person cannot be travelling behind you, to know that you turn there.

Another problem is turning right from the extreme left lane and turning left from extreme right lane. Why can't these people place themselves in the proper lane before turning? They create traffic jams and slow down the traffic. Many times, just because of these people others miss the crossing and face the red signal.

It is important to prepare a travel plan in advance in your mind, decide what road you would like to take, and where you need to turn, whether right or left and place yourself in the proper lane. It is all right if you are new to a particular place but I see many people making the same mistake at the same place everyday.

When are we going to become aware and start insisting on following/maintaining road safety rules?

What we saw is the case of private vehicles that need to be changed by individual participation and acceptance, but what about public vehicles? Public transport bus drivers/auto drivers and municipal and Government vehicle drivers including the Police think that the road safety rules are not applicable to them as the rules are made for private vehicles. Actually these public service vehicles which are on road all the time should follow rules meticulously and if they break traffic rules they should get at least double the punishment given to private vehicle drivers.

Let us decide to maintain Traffic, sorry, Road safety rules and avoid accidents and tension.

Points to Ponder

1.   Follow traffic rules religiously; they are beneficial to all.

2.   Learn traffic rules properly; a booklet is available in book stores, RTO office and details are available on the internet also.

3.   When the Orange light is on, it is the time when pedestrians normally cross the road. Do not start moving before the light turns green.

4.   Do not move while the pedestrian signal is on as

they have the RIGHT to use the road and one should not take it away from them.

5.   Traffic police are supposed to take action against people breaking traffic rules. It is a cognizable offence and no one is required to complain about it.

6.   Follow lane discipline as it smoothens and speeds up the traffic. By breaking lane discipline, you may save time but become the cause of delay for the rest of the world.

7.   Traffic policemen should insist on lane discipline at crossings and persons in the right lane must be allowed to take 'U' or RIGHT turns only, and persons in the left lane should be made to turn left. When people feel the pinch, they will learn.

8.   Two wheelers are cleared for travel by only two persons. But no one takes action on more than two people travelling on a two wheeler. Traffic police authorities must confiscate the two-wheeler and make the offenders pay fine the next day along with the towing charges. It is found that policemen harass young couples travelling with a baby on a two-wheeler but let go off young men/girls even when more than three people are riding the two-wheeler. You get a feeling that the police are afraid of taking action on young men.

9.   All political parties should dictate to their workers not to break traffic rules. It was a pity that a central minister and CM elect were photographed travelling on a two wheeler without a helmet, when the wearing of a helmet is a rule.

10. Policemen are found taking action against common citizens and allowing all the SUVs and public transport vehicles to break the traffic rules (They are afraid after an MLA in Maharashtra who was fined by a PSI for breaking the rules, retaliated by suspending the PSI. The same MLA was given a ticket by a national party). Rules should be the same for all the people.

11. All drivers of public service vehicles (buses, autos, taxis and municipal and Government vehicles including police vehicles) should be fined heavily (at least three to four times more than the normal vehicle drivers) along with/or imprisonment and cancellation/suspension of their driving licenses as they are on the road all the time and likely to cause major damages.

12. Unfit Government vehicles are seen plying on the road (buses, municipal vehicles). In such cases, the chief officers of these departments should be punished heavily with personal fine and suspension.

5. Personal Job Responsibility

When a person is studying he/she has many plans on how he/she is going to work hard and grow in the organization at supersonic speed and become a person with recognition and respect in society. There is nothing wrong in having dreams and ambitions. In fact, every person should have dreams and ambitions that will create a drive in them to work hard and achieve success. People without this drive do not ever think of doing something extra, to get something more than what they are getting. These kind of people with a laidback attitude are happy with what they are getting and are more interested in saving their jobs rather than growth. For this reason they will do what is required to ensure that they are not at serious fault. Management is happy with such people for many reasons, for example,

1. These people never think of changing jobs.

2. They do not involve themselves in office/workplace politics.

3. They can be easily frightened to ensure/extract minimum required quality of work.

4. They are friendly and keep the atmosphere healthy,

over a period of time and are respected by their colleagues.

5. They can be used to get information about others.

6. They never get frustrated for not getting promoted, and an extra increment in the salary once in a way keeps them happy and content.

The main problem is from the persons who are neither ambitious nor job-saving types. These are the people who are cribbers. These cribbers think-

1. That they are being wronged by the society by not being given a job which properly suits their abilities and intelligence.

2. Their superior is less capable than them and less intelligent but has secured the higher position by pleasing his superiors.

3. The system is all wrong because -

   a. The system is asking for good scores in academics.

   b. The system is asking for good communication skills.

   c. The system is asking for responsible behaviour.

   d. The system is asking for a good track record.

4. If they get the opportunity they will change the system and show dramatic growth and improvements.

5. Their ideas are never heard and they are ignored.

   These cribbers are found everywhere and because

they are unhappy, they do not do the work they are supposed to be doing and create a bad atmosphere everywhere. These cribbers can be found among -

I.   Sweepers

II.   Auto rickshaw drivers

III. Bus conductors

IV.   Bus drivers

V.   Cleaners on trucks

VI.   Clerks in various organizations

VII. Salesmen

VIII. Supervisors at many organizations

IX.   Mechanics

X.   Teachers/lecturers

XI.   Accountants

XII. Machine and plant operators

XIII. Policemen and watchmen

XIV. And many more other people

Most of them do not know that they are cribbers and are spoiling the atmosphere. They genuinely believe that they have been wronged and they have the right to rebel (not openly) and shun work. What is important for these cribbers and to that effect for everyone, is to do a simple, honest SWOT analysis of themselves and find out -

S - Their Strengths

1. Are they using their strengths to their fullest capacities?

2. Are they getting the right opportunities to show their capabilities?

3. Are they in a position to complete their assigned work in a short time without any mistakes?

4. Have they ever approached their superiors and asked for work of a higher responsibility, without asking for promotions?

5. Are they in the right place of work?

W- Their Weaknesses

6. Do they know what is expected of them in the job they are doing?

7. Are they doing it completely and competently?

8. What qualities do they lack, according to their superiors?

9. Are they in a position to rectify their short-comings?

10. Why is it that their ideas are not heard by the superiors? Are they not practical? Are these ideas properly proposed with enough ground work and cost-benefit analysis to support them?

11. Are they capable of making proposals of their ideas with cost-benefit analysis?

12. Do they not have anyone to help them prepare the

proposals in a proper format?

13. Are they working in a wrong/unprofessional organization where merit is not recognized?

14. Is there anyone who is preventing them from getting promoted?

O- Opportunities

- Is there any vacancy at a higher level?

- Are they qualified for a higher post?

- Can they train/educate themselves to become capable for and be considered for a higher post?

- Can they get any support from their seniors/organization in training/ educating themselves for higher positions?

- Can they apply to the organization and get a higher position/salary?

- Will they be able to get another job with the same salary in case they lose the current job?

- Is there any chance of overcoming all the obstacles that prevent them from being promoted?

T- Threats

- What are the chances of them getting sacked due to their inefficiency?

- What is their chance of remaining jobless after losing their current jobs?

The SWOT analysis will clearly explain to them that either they are not capable of getting promoted or they lack certain qualities to prove their worth (remember that promoting someone who is worthless is like tying a dead weight to your leg and trying to run fast in a professional organization). It is possible that many of these cribbers will not be honest to themselves also and rate themselves high enough (basically that is their main problem) to get promoted and still keep cribbing. In such a situation, it is the superior's duty to counsel them and tell them to behave or quit. Unfortunately, no one takes this step and no one takes disciplinary action against the erring/cribbing employees on humanitarian grounds. Attitude Change Required

- Everyone should accept their fate and do the job which they have, properly and honestly.

- Remember, there are lots of people who are unemployed and willing to do their job for a lot less money also.

- No one is indispensable.

- Keep looking for a job that suits your capacity and capability, if you are unhappy about the job you are doing.

- Keep doing your job properly till such a time that you get a job of your liking.

We always praise countries like Singapore and countries in the western world. But we do not want to follow their work culture. Their people do their jobs sincerely and resign if they do not find their jobs satisfactory. Are we willing to do that? The answer is a big NO. We will not leave the job and search for another because we know that there is no other job available for us. We keep cribbing and spoiling the work and image of our country.

Points to Ponder

1. Love the job you are doing and if you do not like it leave it. Someone else will do it more efficiently.

2. Ask yourself, whether you know what your job responsibility is. If you do not know, get the information from your seniors.

3. Ask yourself a question - are you really capable of doing the job you have been entrusted? If yes, how can you do it so that it will be the best? If not, how can you get the required skills?

4. Be ambitious, but before expecting a higher position prepare yourself for that position by acquiring the skillsets required for a higher position.

5. Keep applying for jobs at a higher level and see if you can get selected. If you can get selected, then resign and join the new job. If not, be satisfied with the position you are working at.

Become responsible for the job you are doing or quit.

6. Law & Order - Policing

Maintaining law and order is a job assigned to the police force, which means they should do the following:

1. Preventive maintenance to ensure that law and order does not get disturbed.

2. All anti-social elements are identified, watched and warned against creating any disturbances.

3. Policemen should make rounds and make their presence felt to all law-abiding and law-breaking citizens, so that the law-abiding citizens will have faith in policing and law-breaking citizens will think twice before breaking the law.

4. If they see any unlawful activity, they should take cognizance of it and act against it on the spot and not wait for someone to make a complaint and file an FIR (First Information Report).

5. They should act in an equally responsible manner with socially and financially weak and strong persons and should not show any bias for the financially strong (may-be because of criminal activities they perform) and take their side in

dealing with complaints.

6. Investigate all the crimes and catch the culprits within a reasonable time and file a charge sheet against them in such a way that they get punished by the court of law.

Now what do we actually see? We see that the policemen are not to be seen anywhere. Even when they are present on the crime scene, they do not take any cognizance of it and if asked to intervene, their standard answer is, "Chowki war chala (come to the police station and make a complaint)" or "I am off-duty or on leave."

No one is interested in leaving their work and going to the police station where they take their sweet time and make you wait for such a long time that you start wondering whether it is worth spending so much time and energy for justice. You are lucky if they do not accuse you of some mischief (the culprits are mostly their friends as they keep coming to the police station regularly for such reasons) and make you feel like a criminal. If you question them, their answer is, "Nowadays, white collar crimes have increased to such a level that you never know who is the criminal and who is not" or they threaten you with detention for creating obstacles in the work of a Government servant. But you see royal treatment being offered to all the goons in police stations (source of additional income, is it?)

Why is this happening? Why are they trying to protect the interests of criminal elements? Not all criminal elements and petty offenders are their informers. They must remember that Dawood Ibrahim was let go while he was doing petty crimes as he was the son of a policeman and then he became so strong and mighty that police officers started fearing action against them from political bosses if they acted against Dawood. This is not an isolated story. There are instances where robbers were caught red-handed were found to be policemen from police stations in another city. Criminals posing as policemen in plain clothes and robbing women of their gold are common and many times these criminals are suspended or sacked policemen.

- Why are we allowing the police force to get degraded?

- Why do policemen not wear distinct uniforms? (Private security men should be prevented from wearing uniforms that look like police uniforms)

- Why do plain clothes policemen on crime detection/local investigation duty not carry distinct identity cards?

- Why is this happening?

Many times the answer given is, "We have inadequate police force."

This answer is not acceptable because when we say that we have 130 policemen for every 1 lakh of population we do not count the State Reserve Police (SRP) and the Provincial Armed Constabulary (PAC) in it. If we count them, we are as good a police force that equals United Kingdom (UK) and United States of America (USA) per lakh population. But we do not use SRP or PAC or home guards for duties like -

1. Escort duty of politicians.

2. Bandobast for visits of politicians/ministers and VIPs.

3. Protection to persons who are assigned various categories of security.

4. Security of Government offices and Courts of law.

5. Security of infrastructure like dams and electrical installations.

We use normal Policemen for these duties, reducing them to less than one fourth of their strength (considering policemen on medical leave). Thankfully, the security of airports has been assigned to the Central Industrial Security Force (CISF) recently or else that was also being done by the normal state police. If we start deploying CRPF/SRP/PAC/home guards for all these activities, we can make the police force free for law and order activities.

Another aspect is why do we need so many policemen in any police station or a police chowki? It is okay to have large numbers present in Naxal-affected areas as they attack the police stations and take away the police arms. But we see that when Naxals attack police stations, it is unguarded and empty and we see police stations in cities crowded by plenty of policemen. Let these policemen go out and make rounds in crowded places like markets, bus stands, movie theatres etc. instead of loitering around the police station.

Last but not the least, why are we not recruiting policemen?

- We have unemployment.

- We have able-bodied qualified persons interested in getting recruited.

- We can collect enough fine from the culprits breaking the law which can fund twice the size of the police force.

Is it political apathy? Or do we not want a crime-free society?

The Other Side

Policemen say that no one listens to their side of the story and that they have their own problems too. Everyone agrees to this point but is not willing to listen because the police department has lost its credibility. The behaviour of a common policeman towards people is very bad. Our law professes that every person is innocent till proved guilty but policemen treat every person as a criminal and say that it is their right to doubt every person and that it is a proven method of solving cases. If it is so, why is their crime-solving record so dismal (less than 10% cases are solved even when all the crimes are not recorded. If all the cases are recorded, the crime-solving record will be less than 1%).

What Policemen Want -

1. Eight hours working per day with one weekly holiday.

2. Respectable behaviour by seniors and politicians.

3. Better amenities at police stations.

4. Better facilities like computers, printers, internet at police stations.

5. Bullet-proof vests, better arms.

6. Better residential accommodation near the police station.

7. Mobiles/wireless phones.

8. Vehicles for patrolling.

Most of the police constables have their own motorcycles and get conveyance allowance regularly. The arms are not kept in protective custody in the police stations and are stolen by criminals/terrorists, and cases of policemen losing their service revolver is common. The furniture in police stations is misused and so gets damaged frequently. There is no responsible person to take care of office/police station administration (the 'Thane Ammaldar'/SHO is supposed to do so) and the police stations are in bad shape.

Policemen can get everything once they start showing responsible behaviour and earn the respect of the common people.

Points to Ponder

1. Policemen's first and foremost responsibility is to prevent crime.

2. Let us have a separate force for -

- Crime prevention
- Crime detection
- Homicide detection
- Crimes by gangsters
- Narcotics department
- Forensic and crime records department
- Escort duty to politicians
- Security to endangered people (not criminals)
- Security at the courts of law
- Traffic department
- Highway patrol

3. Let us have the facility to login complaints on the internet.

4. At police stations there should be a good atmosphere, clean and neat places for waiting, good toilets for policemen and visitors.

5. Policemen should prevent crime and not hide crimes (like they do now) by not recording the FIRs.

6. Policemen found involved in crimes should be heavily punished/removed from duty.

7. A portion of the fines collected by policemen should be given to the same police station for their welfare activity.

8. Outsource some of the duties (traffic), if additional policemen cannot be recruited. The fine collected can be used for financing outsourcing.

7.Road Safety Rules for Pedestrians

Many road accidents are happening throughout India where pedestrians are knocked down by speeding (?) vehicles. Many of these accidents are fatal and most of the time, the drivers are blamed for the accidents. Is it true that every time the driver of the vehicle is at fault? Is it not possible that the pedestrian is at fault? In one of the news items on railway accidents, it was reported that the persons who got killed while crossing/walking on the railway track ignored the whistle given by the train driver and the reason very clearly stated that these people who were mostly young and middle-aged, were talking on mobile phones or wearing earphones and listening to music/radio on the mobile.

Is it possible that pedestrians are at fault in many accidents because they ignore vehicles and the signals/horns given by them?

Is it possible that most of the pedestrians are ignorant of road safety rules? Most of the people will say, "How is it possible? Road safety rules are taught in schools properly, so all of us know them." But the question remains, are we taught the correct rules of road safety?

For example, which side of the road should one walk on when it does not a have footpath? I have asked this question to many and 99% of the time, I get the wrong answer from across all sections of society. All of them say, "On the left side of the road." This is what is taught in school and all the road safety classes, but it is wrong. I have asked even traffic policemen this question and they have answered it wrongly. Whenever there is no footpath, one should walk on the RIGHT side of the road so that you can see the vehicles approaching you and avoid accidents. The new traffic rules also say that one should walk on the right side of the road. Let us look at the benefits of walking on the RIGHT side of the road.

1. You can see the approaching vehicle and save yourself from getting knocked down.

2. Since you see the vehicle and give side, vehicles are not required to honkand so there is less noise pollution.

3. Since you see the approaching two wheeler vehicle and persons riding it, you can avoid chain-snatching that is rampant (two wheeler riders come from behind and snatch chains and vanish, and you have no chance of looking at/stopping the person).

4. Vehicle movement on smaller roads will improve, avoiding traffic jams.

5. The number of road accidents involving pedestrians will come down drastically.

Are you one of them?

This is only one part of the road safety rules for pedestrians but are we following the other regulations?

* Walk on the footpath - 50% of those killed in road accidents are pedestrians

* ALWAYS REMAIN ALERT WHILE ON THE ROAD.

* Walk on any side of the road if there are footpaths.

* On roads having no footpath, walk on the extreme right side facing the oncoming traffic.

* Always use Zebra Crossing, Foot Over-bridge & Subways to cross the road.

* Cross the road when the vehicles are at a safe distance.

* Wear light-coloured dresses at night.

EVEN A LITTLE CARELESSNESS CAN BE DANGEROUS

* Do not cross the road in a hurry or by running.

* Never cross the road in front of or in between parked vehicles.

* It is very dangerous to cross the road at blind corners, turnings, etc. where   you are not visible to the vehicle drivers.

* Do not jump over the railings to cross the road.

* Do not cross the road diagonal

* Cross the road at Zebra crossings only.

One major thing that I have observed and which is true for most women is that they hold the left arm of the child and walk on the left side of the road exposing the child to easy accidents. Because the child is on the road and walks carelessly, sometimes it runs away from the mother and gets knocked down by a passing vehicle. A child should always be on the extreme side of the road. Many times these women are standing on the busy road not holding the children and the children are merrily playing/dancing unaware of the traffic. How can these women be so careless and if something happens they start shouting, "Can you not see the children?" Now who is to be blamed, these women or the driver of the vehicle? BE alert, follow road safety rules and avoid accidents

Points to remember

1. Always walk on the right side of the road.
2. Cross the road only at road crossings or zebra crossings.
3. When walking with small children, hold them by the right hand and towards the safer side of the road.
4. Do not allow children to run on the road; hold them while crossing the road.
5. Do not break rules while travelling with children.

8. RTO - Vehicle Maintenance Regulations

The Road Transport Authority (RTO) has been assigned a job which has a clear objective of avoiding road accidents and to do whatever is required to ensure that. With this objective, the RTO is required to ensure that-

1. All drivers have the required driving skills.

2. All vehicles are road—worthy.

Do persons in the RTO office know their basic objectives? The answer is NO. Ask them their job responsibility and a maximum number of times you will get the following answers:

a. To issue learning license to maximum persons without delay.

b. To issue driving license to maximum persons without delay.

c. To renew driving licenses of maximum persons everyday.

d. To give registration numbers to maximum vehicles everyday.

e. To give road-worthy certificates (passing) to maximum vehicles everyday.

One can see that the understanding of job responsibility is absent in most of the RTO employees, and the focus has shifted from quality to quantity. In fact, the Mumbai High Court issued orders to many RTO offices to stop issuing road-worthiness certificates as they were not having proper facilities to check the road-worthiness of the vehicles. The orders were retracted when the Government of Maharashtra requested the HC and asked them for time to create these facilities. Are we not playing with the life of innocent people? Most of the road accidents involving cars happen as they are unable to see the trucks, tankers and trailers in front of them as these vehicles do not have tail lights and the mandatory reflectors on their body. Many of the accidents of trucks, tankers and trailers happen due to the driver losing control (malfunction of vehicle) over the vehicle. Every time an accident happens, we either blame the roads or the drivers. Why are we not blaming the RTO authorities for giving a license to the drivers without taking the test or giving road-worthy certificates to vehicles without checking (sometimes without physically seeing it)?

What are the RTO regulations about road-worthiness of vehicles of public use under the Motor Vehicle Act 1988 (re-registration is called passing by the common man)?

1. Produce certificate of registration.

2. Produce vehicle for inspection (procedure of inspection not mentioned).

The MV Act does not talk about the detailed procedure of

inspection. It talks about the registration of new vehicles where all the things that are required when a new vehicle is registered (passed) are mentioned. Here also, most of the people purchase the vehicle from standard manufacturers, who ensure that they are abiding by rules and regulations and get the body also built from standard contractors who know all the regulations. So the problem is not at the time of new registration and the RTO authorities blindly sign the papers. But the main problem is at the time of re-registration (normally done every six to 12 months, depending on the age of the vehicle). At most of the RTO offices the inspection is said to be done by the agents and RTO authorities merely sign saying that they are pressed for time.

Who is forcing them to do more than what they can physically do, thus sacrificing quality?

Let the Government appoint more RTO Inspectors (it will reduce unemployment). RTO offices are self-financed and they actually earn revenue for the Government and therefore the Government can increase the number of offices and staff, without having any problem (except land acquisition). Let us use technology to inspect the vehicles for their road-worthiness. This can ensure that vehicles getting passed are absolutely fit and road-worthy.

If the issuing of road-worthiness certificate is done properly, there will be no need of surprise checks on roads for checking the vehicles. The only problem that remains is the number of vehicles that have been scrapped officially but are running on the road without registration and the number of vehicles having the same number plates. Obviously, only one of them is officially registered. There are a number of news reports talking about unregistered vehicles plying on the roads including taxis, autos and trucks (mostly for supply of building materials, vegetables and water tankers)The RTO inspectors can refuse re-registration (passing) under the following conditions -

4.23 Refusal of registration or renewal of the certificate of registration. (MVAS 45)-

(1)   The registering authority is empowered to refuse to register any vehicle, or renew the certificate of registration of a non-transport vehicle if,

    (a) It is a stolen motor vehicle

    (b) The vehicle is mechanically defective

    (c) The vehicle fails to comply with the requirements of the M.V. Act and rules.

    (d) The applicant fails to furnish previous registration particulars or furnishes inaccurate particulars in the application for the registration of the vehicle.

(2) After refusal of registration, a copy of the refusal order, together with the reasons for such refusal, is required to be given to the owner. It will be interesting to know how many vehicles were denied passing for these reasons (statistics provided by the RTO on their website is silent about it).

The conditions of Municipal and other Government department vehicles is miserable as many of these vehicles are found to not have been re-registered for many years and even the state transport and municipal buses are also found to not be road-worthy. I have a feeling that 100% of the garbage collecting vehicles are not road-worthy. Can we not expectat least that the Government and semi Government vehicles be completely road-worthy?

Let us put pressure on the Government to open more number of RTO offices and ensure that the vehicles plying on the road are absolutely road-worthy. This will also generate a lot of employment for the educated unemployed.

Points to ponder

1. Do not issue driving licenses without a proper test being carried out.

2. Do not re-register vehicles in public use unless properly inspected by a responsible officer.

3. Do not issue license badge for drivers of public vehicles unless their criminal record and character is properly verified by a competent authority. Political pressure should not be considered.

4. The Government should open more RTO offices and ask them to become self-sufficient through increase of fees and fines.

9. RTO - License Regulations

Most of the accidents in cities happen due to unskilled drivers who are unaware of the traffic rules, lane discipline etc. Why is this happening?

How are these persons allowed to drive vehicles? These are some of the questions that come to our mind, but do not be surprised as all of these persons have a valid license. How is this possible? Don't worry, everything is possible in this country if you are willing to pay the price!

Most of the people do not want to give a simple test of traffic rules before getting a learning license, so they pay the agent and he gets you a learning license at home. RTO authorities wanted to introduce a driving simulation test that is very common in the USA. But since only 80% of the people appeared for the driving simulation test, public pressure on the authorities increased and the process was abandoned, with the investment on the machines going waste.

- Why can't we be strict about this?

- Why do we get pushed by public pressure?

- Does democracy mean that the public is allowed to

do something that is against the larger interest of society?

The auto rickshaw unions declare that -

- The drivers will not wear uniforms.
- The drivers will not display the badge.
- The drivers will not allow the authorities to check the meter for mal function and tampering.

The Authorities accepted the demands against the public interest because there was political pressure, the minister sided with the unions as it was his vote bank.

Another shocking thing is that when someone's driving license is impounded by the police, the fellow either gets a duplicate license or a fresh driving license. With computers becoming so common, the data is entered to ensure that the same person is not being given multiple driving licenses. But there are cases where truck drivers involved in accidents, have taken fresh driving licenses in different names. How can someone get a driving license with a false identity?

There has to be an end to this misrule. We cannot blame the politicians or the authorities for the same. We need to blame ourselves because we are the people who take pride in procuring a driving license without giving the test. We are the people who take pride in bribing the cops and getting away with driving without licenses. We are the people who take pride in showing off our underage children driving vehicles on the road without a valid license. We are the people who save our underage children speeding on roads without a driving license, when they are involved in serious road accidents and declare the vehicle as stolen or blame the driver for the same.

All these things must stop. The first step would be to begin with the RTO that enforces license regulations, which are accepted by the people. It is here that we must begin to change our attitudes and practices. We can always start issuing driving license in high school/junior college as is done in USA. The mobile driving test simulators can be carried to schools on pre- declared dates. This way, passing the driving examination in the first attempt will become a matter of pride and all the students will spend time and energy to ensure that they know driving and the rules and regulations of road safety.

Points to Ponder

1. Getting a driving license should become difficult, as it will reduce road accidents.

2. The test for awarding license should be in two parts, one part through simulation and the second, on the road by a responsible officer.

3. Driving without license should attract a higher penalty.

4. Getting a duplicate license should become very difficult. One should not get it from any other state in India. The driving license should be linked to the ADHAAR card. The entire data should be linked to all-India grids.

5. Violation of traffic rules frequently should lead to

suspension/cancellation of driving license and if the person is found driving afterwards, the vehicle should be confiscated.

6. Minor rich kids drive vehicles and are involved in fatal accidents. In such cases, the vehicles should be impounded and parents fined heavily, with publicity in the media.

7. RTO license department should become self-financed, the officers and staff should generate their salaries through fees and fines.

8. Giving license badge to taxi/auto drivers should be done properly after checking the authenticity of records produced and proper background checks.

10. Civic Services - Water Supply

Currently, the Middle East is burning as there is a civil war in Libya, Egypt, Iraq, Syria, Ukraine and many other places. Most of it has been initiated by super powers to have a Government that can be remotely controlled by them and thus have control on the crude oil that they produce. It is said that the next world war will be for control on water bodies. India, with abundant rain and many rivers and water bodies that account for more than 20% of the total fresh water supply of the world is careless about conservation and storage of this water. People think that we get rain water free of charge because of the blessings of the Rain God, Indra and so we can use it the way we want it. This attitude has not changed even after most of the people in urban and rural India face water shortage during summers and are dependent on the water supply through tankers. Many cities get water supply one or two days a week in summer. The government and local bodies keep supplying water free of charge at negligible rates to others. Why should it be done? Why can't we charge rates at cost to cost basis if not cost plus basis? If we want service we should be willing to pay for it. Are we not paying for electricity? Are we not paying for transport? Everyone should pay for water and there should be no exemption from it. Table no. 11.1 shows the water rates in India.

Name of city	Rate Rs./kl	Flat rate / year	Rate* 180 l/day *365 days	Per family of 5/year	Amount paid per person/ Day Rs.
Kanpur	2.0		131.4	657	0.36
Indore	2.0		131.4	657	0.36
Surat	2.0		131.4	657	0.36
Madurai	5.0		328.5	1642.5	0.90
Mumbai	4.5		295.6	51478.25	0.81
Pune		1000-2500**			0.82
Delhi	2.66-33.28+			750	0.41
Chennai	2.5-25+	2.5-25+		750	0.41
Bengaluru		15x12=180		15x12=180	0.49
Vijaywada		480		480	0.26
Belgam		720		720	0.40
Gwalior		720		720	0.40
Nagpur		720		720	0.40
Patiala		20 per tap		20 per tap	immaterial
Kanpur		360-1200#		360-1200#	0.40
Gorakhpur		540-1800#		540-1800#	0.40

** Properties having property tax/year below Rs.500 rate are not charged water tax

depending on size of property, + depending on volume consumed

If we start looking at the rates and the agitation that people do (Delhi Govt. toppled on water rates) we feel pity about the Indian people's mentality. All of them spend more money on gutkha/khaini/tobacco, cigarettes, tea/coffee, cinema, wadapav, panipuri, bhel and ice creams. What is the big deal and why are we not willing to pay such small amounts for a facility that is supplied to us regularly after purification and transportation to our individual residences? The amount is less than one outing for watching cinema in any multiplex (there are many who do so at least twice a month) or one outing to any restaurant for having breakfast (not lunch or dinner that costs more and there are families who do it once every week).

I feel the water charges should be at least Rs.1/- per person per day i.e. Rs.1825 per year per family in semi-urban areas, Rs.1.5 per person per day i.e. Rs.2737.5 per family per year in cities and Rs.2 per person per day i.e. Rs.3650 per year per family in metro cities across the board. Misuse of purified water should be stopped by people who use it for gardening, car washing, swimming pools etc. and these people should be charged ten times more rates. This will ensure that people use water sparingly and water shortages will not be faced as a lot of money will be available for conservation, storage and transport of water.

This is one part of the story but what about the inefficiency of the water supply departments? Are they really giving us clean water? Every year we see news reports of water unfit for consumption being supplied through municipal taps. Along with this we see complaints of mixing of sewerage in drinking water because of having rusted pipelines that are laid alongside sewerage pipelines. How many times we are required to call plumbers to clear municipal water pipelines which are choked by plastic bags, and other insoluble material like wood chunks etc. How do these materials enter into drinking water pipes? The water department is careless and inefficient. It is not the people's mistake.

Another major mistake of the Water Supply Department is not having a time-bound programme for replacing old water supply pipelines. Why wait till the pipeline bursts? Why only repair the leakage, why not replace the pipeline? These costs must be included in the cost of water supply. The amount of water that gets wasted must be less than 20% of the total water supply done by the municipal authorities. They must ensure that there is no water seepage and leakage anywhere in the entire water supply grid.

One more problem is unauthorized water connections. To tell you the truth, all unauthorized water connections are given by municipal employees only. The facts that support this statement are that they are the only people who have complete

1. Knowledge of water pipelines.

2.Knowledge of water supply timings to these lines.

3.Knowledge of making a hole in the cast iron main pipes.

4.Digging of roads to pass the new pipelines, which cannot go unnoticed.

Many of the water supply employees are hand in glove with the people who take unauthorized water connections and steal municipal water. Municipal water that has been purified for drinking purpose is being given for building construction purpose in many parts of India. Why are municipal authorities not insisting that the builder use untreated water from bore wells and lakes? Are we charging them industrial rate of supply? I doubt it. Most of them are taking water supply at residential rates.

Third part of the problem is the recycling of used water. The entire sewerage system can be connected to area-wise water treatment plants and the treated water should be used for building constructions, gardening (even municipal gardens use drinking water for gardening), washing cars and automobiles, and washing of roads (washing of roads has been stopped by municipal authorities for many years now). Most of the municipal authorities discharge this water into rivers, thus completely polluting them. Let all the water supply employees understand that it is their responsibility to maintain proper/pure water supply to all the residents in their area, and also ensure that they maintain the water pipelines in good condition to avoid wastage and contamination of water. They should also understand their responsibility in conservation of water and ensure complete recycling and treatment of used water. If we do this, we will never face shortage of water.

Consumers should also change their mentality towards water supply and be willing to pay at least the cost and should not expect charity in the name of welfare.

Points to ponder

1. Proper maps showing water pipeline locations should be available at all ward offices.

2. Enough water should be supplied to all the people at cost to cost basis.

3. Rain water harvesting should be made compulsory in all residential complexes and Government buildings.

4. Recycling of water must be made compulsory, and recycled water should be made available for all non-potable uses (cleaning floors, washing vehicles, gardening, flushing of toilets etc).

5. Availability of running water in public toilets is a must. Only recycled water should be used in public toilets to avoid misuse.

6. No common water connections should be given to slums in cities. Instead, they should be forced to take individual connections and pay for it. If they can spend money on their vices like tobacco/khaini/gutkha and liquor and mobile telephones with ever-changing ringtones, they should also spend money on essentials like water

connections.

7. Supply of free drinking water to everyone (including slums) should be stopped. People must pay for the service they are getting. If subsidy is offered, the authorities should check the total amount that the family spends on mobile phones, movies and vices like gutkha and liquor. If the amount is more than the water bill, the family should not get subsidy on water bill.

11. Civic Services – Cleanliness

'Cleanliness is next to Godliness' is a saying, but all the people in India are bent on remaining human and do not want to earn Godliness. Now there are two main reasons for the dirty environment that is prevalent in all towns and cities and not so much in villages (villagers know that there is no one else to keep their area clean) and they can be listed as follows.

I- Apathy of local Self-Governments

1) Non-availability/not easily accessible garbage dumps in most towns and cities, forcing people to throw garbage in the nearest open space.

2) Regular collection of garbage is absent in most areas of towns and cities.

3) There is no system for solid waste management and its recycling.

4) Unrestricted entry of dogs and manual scavengers in the garbage dumps that creates a mess in and around the garbage dump. We only talk of controlling the stray dog population but need to actually do a lot more about sterilization

of bitches as this is the only solution. If the bitch is sterilized she cannot conceive and give birth to a litter twice a year.

5) There is no supervision of a responsible person on the garbage collection work leading to unhygienic conditions for garbage collectors e.g.

a. No hand gloves are provided to garbage collectors.

b. No safety shoes are provided to garbage collectors.

c. No aprons, uniforms are provided to garbage collectors.

d. No face masks, goggles are provide to garbage collectors.

e. No cleaning facility for garbage collection vehicles even from outside.

f. No assigned place (standing or sitting) for garbage collectors in the collecting vehicle.

g. No canteen facility, washrooms, locker facility and clean environment for garbage collectors at dumping grounds.

1. There is no duty planning and monitoring of garbage collection work.

2. Teams of sweepers for roads, work only part-time and are paid as full time workers, why not make them work full-time and in two shifts? We have plenty of jobless people and if conditions are good, many will come forward to work.

3. Town planners do not provide any place for garbage collection and treatment in town development plans. There are no norms in town planning for it.Fig. The drain was cleaned previous year, but the dirt remained on the footpath for years.

1. When the roads are repaired, and the drains cleaned, the rubble removal contract is not part of the work order. Even if it is part of the work order, the contractor fails to do so and civic authorities release the payments without ensuring that the place is cleaned (they only ensure that their cut is received by them).

II-Apathy of the people

1. People clean their houses but spoil their environment by throwing garbage outside their homes.

2. People expect municipal authorities to come and

clean areas inside their societies and buildings.

3. Because they pay maintenance to the society, they think it is their right to throw garbage outside their homes and it is the responsibility of society to get it cleaned.

4. People do not want to keep garbage ready for collection when the collector comes (it is too early or too late) and are also not willing to keep it at home for the next day's collection. They will throw it out in any open space they see nearby.

5. Throwing of food, cigarette butts and packets, wrappers of food products, empty bottles is not considered as throwing garbage by many people and when confronted, they blame it on small children and visitors doing it.

6. Segregation of waste is not done by most of the people.

7. There is no waste management facility created by most of the housing complexes.

8. Bungalow owners throw all the waste like garden waste and even kitchen waste somewhere nearby because there is facility created for garbage dump by them while forming plots. Owners in the society find paying monthly charges to sweepers exhorbitant.

There has to be a collective effort from both, the people and municipal authorities, and if the municipal authorities provide a clean environment, people will pay for the extra service. But most of the time, municipal authorities promise a clean environment and increase charges but fail to give a clean environment. The increased charges remain as they are and the next time also they increase the charges again without fulfilling promises. The charges keep going up without any cleanliness.

This is in case of residential areas, and when we start looking at the commercial areas, the condition is worse. In commercial areas, the garbage collection should be done at least three times a day but is done once a day, and that too, only in the early morning. The commercial establishments clean their shops and offices in the morning and throw the garbage at a nearby insufficient garbage dump that gets cleared only the next day. Meanwhile, stray dogs have the opportunity to spread the waste further, thus increasing the dirt and mess.

In this case, we cannot blame the commercial units as they are being charged heavily for garbage collection and disposal by the municipal authorities and it is the duty of the municipal authorities to give the proper service for garbage collection.

The third area is of sanitation which also is a part of cleanliness. Municipal authorities fail in this area in all the cities and towns alike. The list is big and is as follows:

I. No urinal/public washrooms provided; or if provided they are inadequate considering the population that is using it.

II. Public toilets and urinals are dirty and have no running water supply.

III. Toilets and washrooms in all the municipal offices are also dirty.

IV. The ducts used for sanitary waste from residential areas and commercial areas are not planned properly, leading to ducts getting choked which overflow creating a lot of inconvenience to people.

V. All the waste is released into the rivers without treating it, creating polluted environments.

VI. Sanitary pipelines of most of the Government buildings are either leaking or broken or no action is taken on it by the Municipal/PWD authorities.

Now what can be done about it? Whenever the point of cleanliness is discussed, Municipal authorities blame the public and for a few days people are harassed and fined for petty offences like spitting in public places. Spitting has two angles to it.

1. Spitting as a habit (tobacco, paan and chewing gutkha/khaini).

2. Spitting because of environmental nausea.

How many times do people spit because of the dirty environment and how many times it is out of habit? You keep the environment clean and the percentage of people spitting will come down drastically and only the habitual spitters will keep spitting and can be fined heavily. Why is it that municipal authorities never introspect and start a real cleanliness drive?Let the local Self-Government people give a clean environment and people will be willing to pay for it, but only after they see results.

Points to ponder

1. All local Self-Government authorities take taxes for maintaining cleanliness and a healthy environment, so they must be made answerable towards it and should be punished heavily for not providing a clean and healthy environment.

2. There should be an annual audit of money collected and money spent on a clean and healthy environment, compared ward-wise and officers should be punished for dereliction of their duties.

3. Every Government office (including the Courts of law) should have an office superintendent who will ensure cleanliness of the office premises, including the toilets.

4. Ward-wise garbage disposal units should be provided and the WardOfficer should be rewarded for running them at 100% efficiency.

5. Ward Officers should be rewarded for making their wards free of stray dogs.

6. All pet owners must register their pets and pay pet-keeping fees to the Municipality, and should be fined heavily if their pets create a nuisance to their neighbors and litter in the open.

7. All dog owners must be compelled to carry shovels, brooms and plastic containers while walking their dogs on the road and should clean the place when the dog passes stools on the road/footpath.

8. Attendance of the sweepers should be monitored by the health officials as it has been found that only

10-20% people on the roll work and others take their salaries without working (after paying cuts to concerned supervisors and officers).

9. All the civic amenities that are taxed should be brought under the Consumer Protection Act and citizens should be allowed to make complaints against civic authorities in consumer courts.

12. Civic Services - Roads

One of the major roles of Civic Services is to provide roads to citizens. But in India, roads have become an area for minting money for the civic administration and the elected representatives. Road tenders come out and get passed, money is paid but the conditions of the roads remain as they are. Political parties win elections on the promise of giving good roads, but the promises remain unfulfilled and again in the next election, the same promises are repeated and people still believe them (for lack of choice). This is a classic example of the saying, 'Public memory is short' and political parties take advantage of the same.

Road maintenance has the following elements-

1. Understanding and deciding the expected usage levels of the roads.

2. Understanding the width, quality and durability requirements of the roads.

3. Quality of construction.

4. Preparing a schedule of resurfacing the roads as

per expected quality depreciation.

5. Resurfacing the roads as per the schedule.

6. Creating a task force for repairing roads for eventual damages because of rains, or digging for any reasons.

7. Prevention of damages to the roads by unauthorized agencies and taking stern action that includes heavy penalty and cost of resurfacing.

8. Creating an effective rain water drainage system that normally damages the roads.

9. Removal of encroachments that reduce the usable portion of the road and increasing the traffic load on it that leads to damages to the overused part of the road.

10. Keeping the roads clean and not allowing dirt to accumulate on it.

Now if we ask the civic administration whether they know these aspects, most of them including the engineers in the road department will say 'NO'. A major problem in almost all the places in India is that the roads are constructed unscientifically and without analyzing the expected and current traffic density. Sometimes, we start doubting the ability of all the civil engineering colleges to teach construction of roads or for that matter any building construction, as the quality of the roads as well as the buildings is very bad (check the dimensions of the windows or walls in any house - they are never perfect quadrilaterals). Unscientific construction and improper maintenance leads to -

- Narrow roads when wider roads are required.

- Lightly compressed roads when road with heavy rollers are required.

- Narrow lanes are concretized when main roads need concrete construction.

- Road crossings are not synchronized, leading to branching of roads at more number of places.

- Flyovers and/or level separators are not created as per the requirements.

- Faulty flyover designs, leading to it becoming useless (more problems created than solved).

- Ring roads are not planned in anticipation of expected traffic growth.

- Road widening is done to settle hawkers (hawkers are allowed but parking is not allowed).

- A major part of the roads is used by the civic departments for storage of junk.

- Footpaths are used by civic authorities as site offices for their various departments.

- Resurfacing and construction priority is decided by the elected representative's nuisance value rather than actual requirements.

- Footpaths are encroached upon by
  i. Hawkers
  ii. Telephone junction boxes
  iii. Electricity junction boxes

iv. Bus stop shades

v. Storage of civic construction and other materials

vi. Shopkeepers nearby

· Though footpaths are fitted with tiles or paving blocks, a number of times in a year, they are in bad shape and are unusable because of the bad quality of construction.

Most of the time when discussions on the condition of roads takes place, we only talk about the following:

Bad quality of constructions

Unauthorized digging of roads by various agencies and people.

Why do we never talk about the following?

Bad planning of roads and flyovers.

Bad supervision of the construction of roads.

Bad quality control of material being used.

No practice of caution money deposits from the road contractors.

Construction contracts being given to contracting firms floated by civic staff and/or elected representatives.

Advances are being given to road contractors at the beginning, when it should not be given before a major part of the construction is done, that too after keeping some amount balance as caution deposit.

Payments are released before quality and

completion reports are received, sometimes even without the work being started. Many civic officials have property worth crores when their known income is in a few thousands.

If we start talking about all these things and put the responsibility squarely on the civic administrative staff and take strict punitive action against them, the road conditions will become good but there will be no staff left to work in the department. It is becoming a practice to blame only the elected representatives when civic staff is equally responsible and should also be blamed.

Road widening

It is found that people are not giving their land for road widening because they are not compensated fully. Many people handover their land in good faith and then civic authorities make them run around to get compensation and are forced to give a large cut for getting the compensation. There should be proper guidelines for compensation and it should be paid promptly.Many times, land is acquired for road widening and then it is encroached upon by squatters and garages, and finally, the road remains narrow. If the land is acquired for road widening, then the road should effectively get widened.

Let us force civic staff to maintain roads in good condition.

Points to ponder

1. Roads and flyovers must be planned by planners who are nationally certified.

2. Contractors must be forced to keep caution money deposit with the civic authorities towards penalty for bad work/warranty.

3. Contractors should not have more than one layer of subcontractors. Normally it has been found that subcontractors appoint sub-sub-contractors and they in turn appoint sub-contractors to do work and the work quality deteriorates without any check.

4. Civic authorities certify all the work sitting in their offices (their own or the contractor's) or liquor bar without inspecting the work physically. They should be heavily punished along with the contractor for substandard work.

5. There should be a fixed calendar of maintenance where civic authorities should keep doing the work within their fixed budget without any sanction required from the civic body. Officers found not doing their work properly should be heavily punished.

6. Civic authorities collect taxes towards creating and maintaining roads, so they should be made accountable for it.

7. All the civic amenities that are taxed should be brought under the Consumer Protection Act and citizens should be allowed to register complaints against civic authorities in consumer courts.

8. People should not be allowed to purchase any kind of vehicles if they do not have the parking space for it. If they use public space for parking, they should be charged heavy parking charges. ◆◆◆◆

13. Civic Services - Street Lights

One of the responsibilities of the Civic Administration is to provide street lights. This practice is historical and in the olden days, kings used to own a lot of land and part of the revenue used to go to the village revenue collector (Khot, Patwari or Kulkarni) to ensure that street lighting was provided in all the villages/towns and cities. The reasons for providing street lights was simple.

- People should be able to see the road.
- People should be able to avoid accidents.
- Movement of thieves can be restricted and identified.
- Criminal activities like mugging and looting can be prevented on roads.

This responsibility was carried out even by the British Government and they ensured that streets lights were provided everywhere. The problem is with the current civic authorities - either they do not understand the basic objectives behind providing street lights or they do not understand how to fulfill the responsibility. For instance, what we see today is

1. The street lights are not properly spaced according to the capacity of the light to illuminate the road space, leaving blind spaces in between.

2. Street lights are placed closer to big trees due to which there is darkness under the tree. The Electricity department does not take pains to cut the tree branches that block the street lights.

3. Maintenance is poor, thus leaving many street lights non-functional and so there are large patches of darkness.

4. Many street light switches are not properly timed and so they are in the ON mode during the day and in the OFF mode during the night.

5. Criminal elements conducting criminal activities ensure that the street lights are not working in the area of their operation. No action is taken to repair these lights and so, taking action against criminal elements becomes difficult.

6. Main roads, where a lot of illumination is available due to the neon signs and bright lights of the shops have lights in good condition and the bad/side roads do not have working lights, so there is darkness.

7. There is no backup for street lights and there are no emergency lights, so if there is power failure in an area and street lights also do not work, then the area goes into complete darkness. Street lights should always have a separate grid of supply.

8. The road signalling system also does not have an

emergency power supply system and when there is no power supply to a particular area, the signals also do not work.

No one can say that there are no funds for improving the system, not one of the civic authorities had applied for funds to JNNURM (Jawaharlal Nehru National Urban Renewal Mission) for improving the street lighting and signalling system in the city. Most of the cities applied for civic transport (purchase of buses), BRTS (Bus Rapid Transit System) metro and roads.

- Why is there so much apathy towards creating and maintaining the street lighting system?

- Do the street light department employees not know or understand their responsibility towards citizens?

- Do we think it is wastage of efforts and money?

- Are the employees of the street light department inadequate in numbers and skills?

- Is the street light department not provided with adequate equipment and spares?

- Do the street light department employees think that they have been appointed for charity work and are not supposed to work?

With higher and higher instances of chain snatching on secluded, poorly lit roads and the thefts that are occurring on these roads, is it not important that the civic authorities give enough importance to the maintenance of the street lights? Molestations and rapes also happen on dimly lit streets. Wake up Street Light Department, the molested person can also be from your family. .

We all expect good maintenance of the street lighting system for a safer life.

Points to Ponder

1. Proper street lighting should be provided by civic authorities.

2. Preventive maintenance should be done periodically. No part of the city should be dark in the night and civic authorities should ensure that all the areas are provided with proper street lighting.

3. Periodic maintenance must be done to ensure that all the lights are in good working condition.

4. Tree branches that create shadows under the street light must be pruned regularly.

5. Civic authorities should ensure that no one is taking unauthorized connections of electricity from street light poles even during festivals like Ganeshotsav or Durga Pooja.

6. Street light poles must be shifted immediately after road widening is done to avoid accidents.

7. Street light poles should not be allowed to be used by cable operators for running their cables.

4. For failures, the concerned officials should be held responsible and punished.

5. Since civic authorities collect tax for providing street lights, failure to do so should be treated as dereliction of duty and they should be punished.

6. All the civic amenities that are taxed should be brought under the Consumer Protection Act and citizens should be allowed to register complaints against civic authorities in consumer courts.

14. Civic Services - Public Transport

Public transport is the lifeline of any city, and is helpful to the city, the public and the nation in many ways. A few of its benefits –are as follows:

1. Reduces the requirement of private vehicles and so reduces the number of vehicles on the road.

2. Reduction in the number of vehicles leads to reduction of fuel requirement and so saving of precious foreign exchange.

3. Reduction in the number of vehicles on the roads reduces the pollution levels in that place.

4. Reduces the requirement of parking places in commercial areas.

5. Reduces the number of accidents and the disability of people.

6. Reduces the number of deaths due to road accidents.

7. Reduces the show of inequality.

8. Creates more jobs in the public transport system.

9. Increases revenue to the civic bodies.

10. Makes the life of people tension free.

With all these benefits, why is it that we do not have a good public transport system? Is it true that the two wheeler automobile companies are bribing elected representatives and civic officials to ensure a bad public transport system so that they can sell more vehicles?

If we start looking into the problems of the public transport system, we find the following:

The public transport system is always a loss-making venture for civic administration.

Public transport employees are unionized and they go on strike and create problems for the public.

Some people argue that the public transport system is a drain on civic resources, then why not allow private companies to run public transport? The best bus service in India is between Mangalore and Udupi which is run by private operators. There is no overcrowding in the bus, the buses are clean and in good condition, everyone gets a ticket, the staff is well-behaved. What else do you want? The bus service in Tamil Nadu is similar. The State Government has three-four companies along with another ten by private operators. One can travel in any part of Tamil Nadu in the bus very comfortably (only tall people like me are a little uncomfortable). All these companies are profitable. Why is it that when the civic service is running, the bus service is unprofitable? In a city like Pune the civic bus service is perennially in loss even after charging bus fares that are one of the highest in the country (actually it is cheaper to travel by auto in Pune when three people are travelling, rather than travel by PMPL).

Something is wrong somewhere. If the civic administration is unable to run the bus service properly, it should be given out to private companies and not to one operator but to three/four operators and let them compete with each other. They will run the service better and still be profitable. It would be best not to give them the monopoly, for if they are given monopoly for any area, the service will be bad.

Create a good public transport whether it is bus service, local train, mono or metro and run them efficiently and people will not use their own vehicles. In Singapore where you see the best of public transport (buses, mono rails/ metro rails and shuttles), the administration has very strict rules on the purchase of vehicles and maintaining them. So very few people can afford to purchase and use private vehicles. The public transport though comparatively cheaper, is not subsidized. It runs commercially and is still in profit.

Let us hope that civic authorities come out with solutions for running public transport efficiently and profitably. No one will then mind whether it is public transport or private parties running the show.

Points to ponder

1. Ensure that buses are maintained in proper road-worthy condition all the time. No bus should be allowed to ply on the road if it is not road- worthy.

2. Maintenance staff should also work in shifts (three

shifts) to ensure that buses are well-maintained.

3.Strict control on spare parts should be maintained and thefts should be avoided.

4.Public workshops are famous for replacing new spares with old ones and selling the new parts in the market, and this should not be allowed at all.

5.Civic buses become old in less than one month as their new parts are removed and sold to make money. It should be ensured that this does not happen.

6.If there is a breakdown of a bus on the road, the depot manager should be held responsible for it along with the maintenance supervisor and punished for dereliction of duty.

7.Services to loss-making routes should be curtailed and if the civic councillor/corporator asks for additional services, the loss should be covered from his ward welfare amount.

8.Mini buses should be used in areas where less passengers are available and can be without the conductor (the driver would issue tickets).

9.Mini buses should be used in areas where roads are narrow.

10.All concessions (except school concessions) should be stopped. This will reduce losses and also unnecessary travel.

11.The ticket charges should be based on actual expenses. If people cannot afford the ticket they should walk or travel by cycles. (When people can spend lot of money on their vices and cinema theatres why should they get concessions on bus tickets?)

12. Buses should be cleaned and washed every day, and recycled water should be used for the purpose.

15. Civic Services - Maintenance of Open Spaces and Roads From Encroachments

Encroachments are becoming a major problem in all towns and cities. There are many possible reasons why encroachments happen. We can list them as follows:

1. There is no one to stop encroachments and timely removal of encroachments.

2. Civic staff is more interested in taking bribes from encroachers, than in removing them (it becomes a source of regular income).

3. Policemen take action on parking in the no parking zone but allow encroachments, saying that they do not have authority, but take bribes from the encroachers.

4. There is no fixed policy towards encroachments.

5. Under political pressure many encroachments are legalized.

6. Many encroachers pay rent for the place they are occupying to the local goon/elected representative and in addition, keep paying daily fees to the civic

administration and bribes to civic staff and policemen.

7. Encroachers take unauthorized water and electricity connections by paying bribes to the respective staff.

8. Allowing encroachments has become a source of additional income to staff members of the civic administration, electricity staff, policemen and local goons. So the encroachers are welcomed by them, while citizens who get affected crib.

9. Citizens purchase a lot of products, vegetables and fruits from encroachers because they think they are saving money (actually they are not) and efforts to travel up to the shopping complexes.

10. Citizens want street hawkers, and at the same time do not want them - as per their convenience.

After looking at the reasons for encroachments let us look at the various places that get encroached upon.

- Roads and footpaths.

- Open spaces owned by various Government departments.

- Private open spaces lying unused.

- Open spaces earmarked for play grounds and civic amenities.

- Canals and storm water drains.

Fig. Do we widen the roads for this purpose?

Now let us look at the reasons why they are being encroached upon.

- Migrant settlers leading to slums development.
- Hawkers.
- Shopkeepers - for additional utility space.
- Construction of shops and garages.

What needs to be done is the biggest question, because many people know about why, how and where the encroachments are but no one comes up with solutions. Stopping encroachment, maintaining the roads and open spaces is definitely the responsibility of the civic administration. We keep blaming the elected representatives for regularizing the encroachments but regularizing comes later. If encroachments are not allowed in the first place and removed immediately before the encroacher settles firmly, (creating contacts with local elected representatives and goons) then that is best for everyone.

There has to be a method of fixing responsibility on the civic staff and strict punitive action that includes fines and removal from service needs to be incorporated. Unless the civic staff is penalized, encroachments cannot be stopped.

Points to ponder

1. Hold the ward officer responsible for every encroachment and punish them for it (they know all the encroachments as they collect bribes from encroachers.)

2. Instead of giving free re-settlement to slum dwellers, create cheap housing in advance and force them to go and stay there (rental/ownership). Evict them from the slums and do not allow them to encroach upon Government/private lands.

3. Do not provide civic amenities to encroachers even on humanitarian grounds.

4. In most shopping areas, the parking on the roads is blocked by the shopkeepers and their staff, and there is no parking space left for the customers. These shopkeepers, their staff and residents in those buildings should be forced to park their vehicles in the parking spaces inside the buildings, by vacating them of encroachments (mostly shops and ware-houses of the shopkeepers).

5. Provide parking places in all areas on hourly, daily and monthly basis for people not having parking at their residence/office/commercial establishments.

6. All parking lots should have clean and neat washrooms.

7. If people can purchase a vehicle they should be ready to pay for parking it.

8. Provide cheap rental residential areas on the outskirts of cities/towns to avoid the development of slums. These places should be rented to migrant people on producing work details/AADHAR cards. They should be vacated when they are able to buy/rent a place in a decent location (no sub-tenant should be allowed).

16. Electric Supply

Some weeks ago at about eight in the night, there was a big blast in a nearby society and the power supply went off. The blast had happened in the transformer of that society. The power supply was routed through this society to the entire area and all the people had to remain in the dark for the next 20 hours. The reason was that the power supply people do not do any repair work during the night and their morning starts only after 10.30 am. This situation leads to the following questions:

1. Why are they not working during the nights (most of the complaints will be during the night only)?

2. Why should they start working at 10.30am and not at 7 am like the morning shift of manufacturing organizations?

3. Why are they not doing preventive maintenance of transformers?

4. Why is there no system of supplying power through alternate lines?

5. What about the damages caused to household instruments (TV, fridge, washing machines, music

systems etc.) because of abrupt fluctuations and power shut off?

The electricity supply staff has gone into a situation where they think that they are obliging people by giving power supply. This is similar to the way nationalized bank employees still behave, even after losing business to service-oriented banks. We do not have a system where customers can choose the power supply company. (Unless and until we become a power surplus nation, this won't be possible. In Mumbai, BSES, BEST and MSEDCL are competing with each other but the situation is no better).

Classically, the Electric Supply Department cannot say that they fall short of funds as all the funds they require are being collected at the time of giving the power connections. For example, they take the following amounts before the power supply is given:

1. Cost of the cable from the nearest supply point.

2. Cost of laying the cable from the nearest supply point (digging the road, laying the cable, resurfacing the road and connecting to the distribution point [DP]).

3. Cost of the transformer and its installation.

4. Security deposit for repairs and maintenance of transformer.

5. Security deposit from each and every user towards fixing of meters and their repairs.

6. Actual cost of usage and profit thereof.

7. Taxes and surcharges on the cost of usage.

8. Service charges on the cost of usage of power.

9. Increased security deposits which are taken, without giving any reasons from time to time.

10. Penalties for thefts of power in any area from others who are regularly paying the bills.

So after taking so much of money from the customers, the only expense the electric supply company incurs is the salaries of the people and maintenance cost of the office establishment and instruments. And there can be no funds problem that they face, so any argument in support of service deficiencies is really not acceptable.

What are the different problems faced by the consumers? We can list them as follows:

1. Fluctuations in voltage.

2. Power going off any time of the day and night.

3. Power off every week for maintenance, but no maintenance work is carried out leading to frequent power cuts.

4. Open DPs without lids which can be dangerous and lead to accidents.

5. DPs placed on footpaths blocking the walking space.

6. Power bills being received late, making them ineligible for immediate payment and depriving consumers of discounts offered for paying early.

7. Hanging wires in high density residential areas

leading to accidents.

8. No control (actually many times abetting power thefts) on power thefts.

9. Faulty meters, leading to inflated bills.

10. Above average billing by billing agencies, leading to disputes and loss to consumers.

All these problems are controllable by improving the maintenance of equipment and having the proper attitude of PAID SERVICE PROVIDERS and not Free Service givers.

Every service provider is supposed to have customer service centres (central or area-wise) and have accessibility to the customer complaint mechanism (the numbers of the power supply company are always engaged because they remove the cradle of phone and keep it aside). There should be a facility to inform the customers about any fault in service and the likely time that it is going to take for repairs. The use of computers can help in creating all these facilities.

Points to ponder

1. Since electricity is a paid service (there is no subsidy for urban users, and in fact they are charged more to recover subsidies given to the urban poor and rural electrification), users should get uninterrupted electric supply all the time.

2. Failure to supply uninterrupted electric supply should lead to penalty for electricity boards and

reimbursements to consumers based on the number of hours that no supply was given.

3.Household instruments getting damaged due to fluctuations in load should be fully compensated.

4.Theft of electricity should be treated as a serious offence and should lead to imprisonment along with fines.

5.Transformers are fitted in many locations and their cost and maintenance charges are recovered from the consumers, but these transformers are never serviced properly, thus leading to transformers getting burnt. The officers concerned should be held responsible and severely penalized.

17. Legal System

The Legal System in India is based on the British system wherein the law enforcement agency has to prove that a person has committed a crime. The system worked well during the British Raj when the Indian people's mentality was law-abiding and God-fearing. Today, when people take pride in breaking the law and use God's name for personal advantages, it is clear that the system has stopped working. Witnesses change their statements arbitrarily by taking money, lawyers are bribed for not pressing charges against the accused properly, and policemen are bribed to keep loopholes in their investigations and delaying the filing of charges beyond the 90 day limit. Now there are alleged bribery cases against the Supreme Court and High Court judges and scores of magistrates, so how the legal system is surviving is a big question. In our country, even the President of India, Dr. APJ Abdul Kalam was served with an arrest warrant under section 420 (cheating & forgery) by an Ahmedabad court. The lawyer who got it issued said, "I wanted to show that the legal system in Gujarat is rotten with corruption." He was let off and on top of that, the magistrate who issued the arrest warrant was also not punished. At least the magistrate who signed the arrest warrant should have been given life imprisonment.

There are various points that need to be discussed about the maintenance of the legal system in its pure form. Some of them are -

1. Changing the laws to suit current situations, as many of the laws and legal procedures have not been updated since the British rulers first introduced them in India. In fact, many of them have been made by the East India Company also. The CrPC (Code of Criminal Procedure) 1898 was amended in 1973 and again in 2013 but still has many procedures and acts which are unchanged. For example, the Evidence Act 1873 is still in force and the amendment bill prepared in 2003 has not been passed by the parliament because our law makers do not want to plug the loopholes that help criminals go scot free.

   Why can't we accept the evidences as collected by the policemen under CCTV observation at the crime scene? (If we do not believe our policemen then why do we not change them/admonish them/punish them?). Why don't we have a specialized team for investigating the crime scene (CSI)?

   I.   Allowing criminals to fake sickness and remain in A/C hospital rooms enjoying their lives.

   II. Allowing criminals to come out on parole at will and enjoy their normal life.

III. Allowing criminals to move in their own cars without hand–cuffs instead of the police van (the police say that they had no van and so they use private vehicles).

IV. People charged with murder roam around freely on bail as long as they want to, even when there are eye-witnesses to the murder.

V. Allowing people charged with Goonda Act or Terrorist Act to roam around freely on bail as long as they want.

VI. The criminals involved in serious offences are allowed to get bail and roam freely till they are pronounced not guilty.

The rules must be changed according to the current social situations and all loopholes should be plugged.

2. Changing the classification of the courts that are currently divided into only civil and criminal courts and they should be subdivided into-

Criminal Side

I.   Traffic offences

II.   Accident claims

III.   Thefts

IV.   Robberies

V.   Murders

VI. Cyber crimes

VII. Frauds of a serious nature

VIII. Banking frauds

IX. Insurance claims

X. Crimes against women

XI. Dowry related cases

XII. Atrocities against lower castes

XIII. Criminal intimidation of people (Goonda Act)

XIV. Criminal trespassing

XV. Kidnappings and abductions

XVI. Anti-corruption cases against public servants

XVII. Terrorist activities

XVIII. Crimes against the nation

Civil Side

I. Cases of land ownership

II. Cases of monetary transactions

Family Courts

I. Divorce cases with mutual consent

II. Divorce cases involving alimony

III. Divorce cases where custody of the children is involved

Let all the courts be separated and let us have magistrates and lawyers who specialize in these matters Once these courts are separated and specialized magistrates and lawyers are present, the court cases will get cleared early and the people's faith in the legal system will be revived. Remember that justice delayed is justice denied. Currently, denying justice by delay has become the rule of the nation.

3. Change the justice system completely to suit the citizens so as to ensure that the lawyers do not take the litigant on a ride to make money.

When the Bhopal gas tragedy happened in December 1984, a plane load of USA lawyers reached Bhopal the next day looking for an opportunity to earn money in commission from the people affected, by getting them compensation from the Union Carbide Company. Our legal system did not allow them to file cases against Union Carbide and all those people were deprived of their legal claims of compensation. Most of the victims have still not received any claims and the case has been closed. We must bring in such a legal system where the victims are not troubled by law authorities and not required to attend court a number of times just to get another date and keep paying the lawyer fees, which are many times more than the expected compensation. Ultimately, the court earns court fees, the lawyers earn legal fees and both, the victims and the accused lose lots of time, energy and money.

Because of the system in USA, all the people there are afraid of breaking the law and the citizens are safe. The citizens can also sue any Government department if they are not serviced properly, and can even sue law enforcement agencies if they are found to be breaking the law.

4. Changing the atmosphere of the law courts into a citizen-friendly one where people should not fear approaching the court of law.

Why don't we have an atmosphere where normal citizens can enter the courts of law to watch court proceedings? Why should one start feeling as if he/she is a criminal? The relatives of lawyers, court staff and judges also do not find it good to visit their relatives in the court compounds. The lawyers ask you to meet them in their offices early morning or late evenings. The court staff will ask you to wait outside the court building, in some restaurant and come and meet you. The judges say that they are not authorized to meet anyone while in court. Are they trying to hide something from others or is the atmosphere so bad that they do not want others to know about it?

Why is there no special entry and exit point for policemen carrying under trial criminals? Why is there no special enclosure for under-trial criminals where their relatives and other gangsters are unable to meet them? Why should the policemen

allow criminals to mix up with normal citizens? Why are they not handcuffed and kept separately? How many times do we allow criminals to meet their relatives and unofficially exchange things, including weapons and mobile phones? How many times will we allow them to plan their next criminal act in the court house premises? And how many times will we allow rival gangsters to kill undertrial criminals in courthouse premises? And how many times will we allow criminals to run away from the courthouse?

We must change the system and ensure law and order even in the courthouse premises.

5. Better buildings with hygienic environment.

Most of the court buildings are old and dilapidated, and have been constructed during the British rule, so these buildings have the right to be dirty, unhygienic and smelly, but even the newly constructed multi-storied courthouses are filthy with cobwebs all over. There is no sitting arrangement and if the benches are present, they are shattered and are useless, the washrooms are without running water and never cleaned. I have a feeling that all the civilized lawyers and court staff must be affected by kidney stones and constipation with piles because they cannot go to the washroom for the entire day. Why can we not have an administrative department specially created for each courthouse, which shall ensure that the buildings are in good shape and their upkeep is proper,?

6. Parking space—No Government office has enough parking space and court houses are no different from them. I do not understand why open spaces in Government offices are not paved properly and parking spaces demarcated for the use of judges

(for them, there is separate enclave), lawyers, policemen and litigants. Why can't they start a pay and park system so that vehicles are not parked haphazardly blocking all the carriage ways? There are so many instances where the criminals have run away from courthouses and policemen were unable to catch them because their vehicles were blocked by unruly parking.

Points to ponder

1. There should be separate buildings for criminal/family/civil/small causes/economic offences.

2. An adequate number of judges/magistrates should be appointed to man an adequate number of courthouses.

3. Lawyers should be allowed to rent chambers (of various sizes) in the court premises.

4. All courthouses should have a hygienic environment.

5. People found spitting/urinating in the premises should be directly imprisoned for a day.

6. There should be enough parking spaces in the court premises.

7. Entry/exit points for judges/magistrates, criminals accompanied by policemen and others should be provided separately.

8. There should be a separate enclosure on each floor

for criminals along with policemen.

9. Clean and neat large canteens and restaurants should be available in courthouse premises.

10. Enough number of clean and neat washrooms should be available in the premises.

11. Proper electronic display boards should be made available to declare case numbers along with court room numbers and the expected time of hearing.

18. Education System - Primary

The Primary Education System in India can be called as the most ancient and best as compared to many other countries. There are many people who are concerned about their children's education and take keen interest in teaching their wards at home also along with the school so that he/she is ahead of their class and does not find it difficult in understanding the things that are being taught in the class. The conventional system of children revising the tables to make their base for arithmetic strong and by rote learning and reciting various prayers every day to make their memory strong and pronunciations proper, ensures that the students do well in Maths and Science. This helps them develop their careers in the right directions. Cursive writing was another area that was given a lot of importance and during British rule many people were employed in Government jobs just because their handwriting was excellent. The schools were mostly run by education-oriented people and they took pride in getting the maximum number of their students in the state merit list for fourth standard (scholarship examination).

Then came the system where the Government thought of

extending education to all the people and started opening up schools everywhere under the management of the local Self-Government. The teachers in these schools were appointed by the local politicians. These politicians were interested in appointing candidates who would help them increase their clout in society to further their political interests and not the candidates who have an interest in teaching. These teachers were interested in pleasing their political bosses rather than acquiring skills of teaching and ensuring that their students learn the subjects and get into merit lists. Students passing out of these schools were not accepted in private high schools as they were found to be wanting in many areas. Many high schools asked them to repeat a class before they were admitted to the high schools. This had a two way effect and the Government then decided to take only the trained teachers in their schools to improve the education standard. Many politicians then opened up shops of training colleges where these teachers were being trained. Actually training the teacher was not a problem, an interest in teaching was the problem. But instead of taking action on the cause, the action was taken on the symptom and the quality of education remained at low levels. The teachers said that they were teaching well but the students were not interested in learning and so they made sure that the students did not drop out and remained in school. The plan to motivate the parents and children was as follows:

1. Give free uniforms and books to the students enrolling in the schools.

2. Give these students free mid-day meals.

3. Ensure that all the students pass every year and go to the next standard. To do so, cancel all the examinations in primary schools (up to the fourth standard).

The quality of learning of the students did not go up but three areas of corruption were opened up for the politicians. To ensure that they made a lot of money, the student enrolment and attendance was increased. The more the students, the more was the requirement of uniforms, sweaters, raincoats, mid-day meals and more the bills for passing and more the commission for the politicians. The Quality of Education is still not going up as the students and teachers are absent from schools, and no one is interested in teaching and learning, but the Government is spending a lot of money on primary education.

Is the primary education good in private schools? The answer is yes, to a large extent barring few schools opened up by politicians who take advantage of the absence of fee control and the number of students being enrolled in one class.

Ask them why they have opened these schools. The answer is simple and political, "To ensure that the large masses have a chance to enroll their wards in good private schools, as the current schools are dominated by the upper class and they deny admission to students from socially lower classes."

The real reason is that the opening of a new school is being regulated by the Government, so not many schools are opening. All the schools have gone in for double shift and admission to schools has become difficult. These new schools opened by politicians started asking for donations for admitting students and it has become a good business proposition. Old schools which were forced to give Government-approved salary scales went in for grant-in-aid from the government and so were allowed to take donations or increase the fee structure, but new schools could ask for donation for infrastructure, building and charge high fees.

But has this improved the education? The answer is NO because the number of students per class is nearly 100 and it is not possible for any teacher to focus on every student even if they are really interested in doing so. Now if you are unable to give education, at least create an atmosphere and show a high level of learning. The primary students are being asked to do many projects that even some of the teachers cannot complete, so many students do not submit these projects and students whose parents are interested in getting higher grades for their ward, do these projects themselves or purchase readymade projects from nearby shops and submit them. Now the teachers have a reason for blaming the student for not learning. Students are forced to join extra-curricular activities like drawing, painting, dance and singing, but these activities are never done as the faculty for these activities comes only for inauguration and since the school is not willing to pay the amount demanded, they do not come. Money from the students is collected already and goes into the school profits. Is the student becoming smart? The answer is again NO. The activities that are important and were done religiously earlier have stopped completely. These students are not asked to read any lesson loudly in the class (their stage fear develops, and pronunciations never improve). They do not recite the poems or the tables loudly in the class (they now need a calculator for doing 2+2). Cursive writing has been stopped completely and we hardly find anyone with a good handwriting. The reasoning seems to be that now they are going to use computers when they grow up, so why is good handwriting needed? But what about their education up to graduation and post-graduation where they are required to write the examinations?

What do we need to do?

Allow any number of private schools to open and charge whatever fees they want to collect but on a monthly basis and let the parents decide where their ward should take admission. If the quality is good, students will stay or shift to the school that is giving 'value for money' education. The schools that are not giving good education will get closed automatically for want of students (this is already happening in the case of nursery/pre-primary schools).

Allow schools to use grounds on a sharing basis. These grounds can be private grounds or Government open spaces whenever required. As it is, parents do not want physical activity for their wards other than assembly and some mass PT that can be done in the school stilt area on the ground floor. Insist on qualified full-time teachers and not part-time teachers who are being paid according to the salary scales set by the Government. The teachers must be in the ratio of 1:30 as compared to the number of students. Let the school conduct examinations if they want, and promotion of the students to a higher class, or repetition in the same class can be decided by the parents in consultation with the Class Teacher and the Principal. NO automatic promotion of all the students should be allowed.

Encourage schools to use the internet (free internet may be provided) and projectors so that children can be shown birds, animals, fruits flowers, trees, mountains etc. in their natural conditions and colour and to bring a better understanding in them. Reading, recitation of stories, poems and arithmetic tables should be made compulsory. Cursive writing, drawing and painting should be a part of the curriculum.

Students should not be made to carry many books and should be allowed to keep their school bags at the school. Whenever there is homework, only that book should be carried home by the student. Behavioural Sciences must become a part of the curriculum. Students should be taught to respect elders and teachers (this is already absent in many students). Check whether the teacher teaching this subject is has good mannerisms. Teach only the universally acceptable manners and not what the teacher thinks is RIGHT.

Points to ponder

1. Schools should be free to charge any amount of fee but should be taxed if they are making profits

beyond a fixed limit.

2. Parents should choose schools that they can afford and should not fight with schools over the fee structure.

3. Municipal schools should be available in every ward and those who cannot afford private schools should send their wards to the municipal school and fight with the civic authorities for good facilities.

4. Having no examination till the eighth standard is simply foolishness. If students are unable to pass the exams, penalize the teachers and ask them to improve their teaching.

5. Objective questions should only be used sparingly and there should be more of explanatory, descriptive and application based questions.

6. Physical education and hobby classes should be made compulsory.

7. Participation in Inter-school tournaments for various subjects like elocution, quiz and various sports must be made compulsory to all the schools.

8. Junk food and soft drinks should be banned in the school premises.

9. Compulsory physical fitness should be undertaken for each student and parents should be counselled if the child is not physically fit.

10. Parent-teacher meetings should be regularly held.

19. Education System - Secondary

Secondary Education now starts from the 5th standard onwards, whereas earlier, standards 5th to 7th were called middle school and secondary school or high school started from the 8th standard onwards. The new norms show class 1 to 5 as primary, class 6-8 as upper primary and 9-10 as secondary. But for this book, the author has considered secondary as 5th to 10 th standards/classes. The Secondary Education system is supposed to be governed by either SSC (Secondary School Certificate) boards set up by the State Governments or by CBSC (Central Board of Secondary Certification - Central Government ruled) or ICSE (Indian Certification of Secondary Education - a privately run organization based on the new Education Policy, 1986 in English medium). The curriculum is designed by these respective boards and schools opting for a particular board need to use books recommended by these boards. The educational pattern is governed by these boards but the examinations for standards 5th to 9th are taken and assessed by schools and the final examination of the 10th standard is taken by these boards. Students opting for CBSC and ICSE are spared the compulsion of learning the local language and can move from one state to another without any changes in the education system, so parents having transferable jobs prefer CBSC and ICSE schools.

The curricula are mostly similar to each other as the basic principles of Science, Mathematics, Social Science, Geography and Grammar (all the languages) cannot be interfered with. The political interference comes when the lessons (both prose and poetry) in languages and lessons in history are selected for inclusion in the curriculum. The impact of this inclusion in the lessons on students is negligible as most of the students and teachers are looking at it as a part of the examination system and not of impact generation. So all the students forget what they have learned in the earlier standards, and are unable to correlate any place with its historical importance or unable to recite any poetry learned or remember the names of the authors of these prose and poetry lessons. The problem starts with the maintenance of rules regarding the following:

1. Student/pupil to teacher ratio.

2. Minimum qualification for appointment of teachers.

3. Quality of teaching.

4. Completion of syllabus.

5. Physical training and games.

6. Availability of playground.

7. Availability of library with required number of books.

8. Availability of laboratories with the required instruments and specimens.

9. Availability of halls for extra-curricular activities (drawing/dancing/singing/craft etc.).

10. Monitoring system to ensure that teachers and schools are following the set norms.

Student/Pupil Teacher Ratio

According to one survey, the pupil to teacher ratio in many schools is found to be 115:1 as against the Government set norm of 30:1 in primary, 35:1 in upper primary and 40:1 in secondary, and in the villages it is ONE TEACHER per school with as many students as possible (ranging from 40 to 300). Ideally, the pupil to teacher ratio should be 40:1 but it can be diluted to 50:1, inclusive of the teachers for PT and extra-curricular activities. What happens when a less number of teachers are available? To understand this problem one must understand the teacher's activities that can be listed as follows:

- Prepare lesson plan.
- Teaching the syllabus in such a way that everyone understands it.
- Revise the syllabus to ensure that no one forgets what was taught.
- Take class tests on each lesson taught.
- Give homework for revision at home.
- Correct homework books and give comments.
- Ask to repeat if not done properly and correct the homework again.
- Take mid-term oral and written examinations.
- Assess the answer sheets for mid-term examinations.
- Take term-end examinations.
- Assess the answer sheets for term-end examinations.
- Prepare the result sheet.
- Declare the results and talk to the parents about the progress of their wards.
- Take part in extra-curricular activities like various ceremonies and gatherings.

To do all these activities properly, one needs a lot of time and it is not possible to do so in the free periods. That means carrying the homework books/answer sheets home, with a minimum travelling time of 1 to 1.5 hours one way. Teachers spend around three hours travelling in cities and work eight hours in schools, which totals up to eleven hours per day. If we consider eight hours of sleep and two hours for household chores, the teacher is left with only three hours per day for checking homework books twice a week and answer sheets every three months. No time is left for family and relaxation or entertainment and extra reading. Considering that more than 50% of the teachers are females, they have an additional responsibility of cooking and rearing children. I do not blame the teachers if they are not doing their duty properly.

The blame is not even on the school authorities as in many cases the parents force them to admit more number of students and the Government authorities keep allowing them to do so. The reason behind this is simple. If the pupil to teacher ratio increases, the school authorities will increase the fees and parents are not willing to pay higher fees and also not willing to enroll their wards in municipal schools, where education is free. More schools cannot be opened for want of space availability and funds (restrictions on fees to be collected) and parents insist on English medium private schools.

What is the answer to this problem? Increase the number of books and notebooks and ask the parents to do the job of the teacher. For example,

- There can be a workbook for every subject and the

parents can be expected to ensure that their ward completes the given portion on time (homework correction is not required).

- Give project work to be done at home (not by the parents, but under their supervision.).

Without such steps, if parents are unable to get these done then teachers start blaming the parents for ill progress of the pupil and parents are unable to question the teacher's short–comings.

Minimum qualification for appointment of teachers -

Minimum qualifying mark for secondary teachers is graduation (B.A./B.Sc/B.Com) with at least 50% marks (relaxed to 45% for BC/OBC/SC/ST/NT etc.) along with B.Ed. with salary to be paid at about Rs.22,000/per month if full-time and confirmed in the post. Even after collecting fees from an excess number of students, the school authorities are not willing to pay the required salary to teachers. What is the way out?

- Appoint teachers on an hourly basis.

- Appoint teachers on a leave vacancy basis.

- Appoint teachers on a temporary basis.

These teachers may not have the required qualification and are willing to work at salaries as low as Rs. 2,000/-per month on the promise of getting a permanent job some day with Government recommended salary, when they get the required qualification and the authorities consider them fit. Many teachers keep working like this for many years (10 to 15 years) and still do not get the job.

Quality of teaching and completion of syllabus

As discussed in point number one in the case of the teacher to pupil ratio, it is impossible to give quality education when so many students are enrolled in one class and so is the case of the completion of the syllabus.

Physical training and games and availability of play grounds

Physical training and games is becoming optional to students in schools, as many schools do not have a proper playground near to the school. On paper, they produce an NOC for the use of the ground facility of some ground where they claim they take the students by school bus. In actual reality the students are never taken to these grounds more than once a year. Wherever a ground is available (though smaller than required), the students are taken to the ground. Many students go in the corner and sit in a group chatting or playing games on their mobiles. If asked to join the games, they say they are sick and that they have been asked to abstain from physical activity. Teachers also do not force them to join fearing repercussion and concentrate on the students interested in playing games. Mass PT is also not done as the ground is small and cannot accommodate so many students at a time. So we have our future citizens physically weak and obese. Incidences of obesity and diabetes in children are increasing at an alarming rate but parents are not bothered and do not force their wards to participate in games and physical activity fearing injuries. Actually they should understand that injuries are part of growing up and becoming strong physically and mentally.

Fig. Physical activity and training should be made compulsory in schools

Availability of a library with the required number of books

The Library period is not given to students at all in many schools and the libraries that are available in school are reserved for teachers only as the number of books (at least one per student enrolled in school) are not available. Students are not being asked to read story books loudly in the class and because of this, most of the students become shy and are afraid of speaking in front of people other than their close group. Students are unable to pronounce many words properly and cannot understand the meaning of many words as their vocabulary is very small. This is true for both, the English medium and Non-English medium schools. Less and less number of school children are interested in reading books and are addicted to television rather than any kind of books. Scientifically, we say that audio-visual presentation has a better impact on the minds of people but it leaves very little to imagination and many times does not attract concentration of the audience. Because of this it is found that when some-one is reading a book with interest as a hobby, their understanding of the subject at hand is much better than that of audio-visual and the recall or remembrance is also much better. It is important that students are put into the habit of reading for their all-round growth.

Availability of laboratories with the required instruments and specimens

Availability of laboratories is becoming a thing of the past and many times even the higher secondary schools do not have this facility. In many schools which were not having laboratories, the teachers used to bring the specimen and/or instruments in the class and show the experiment in the class; but with nearly 100 students in each class, showing the experiment or specimen to all the students has become impossible. Schools can very well go in for projectors and slides/videos but who will invest in them? Most of the students are unable to recognize many objects as they only know their names but have not seen them either physically or in pictures. A subject like computer education is a part of the syllabus for all the schools but even the Principal of the school or the accountant does not have a PC. (Many schools, even after having a PC in the office are not reachable by e-mail as they do not have an e-mail ID or most of the people do not know how to operate the internet. This is true for many colleges also).

Availability of halls for extracurricular activities (drawing/dancing/singing/craft etc.)

Fig. Place for developing and pursuing hobbie

Most of the schools do not have a space specified for extra-curricular activities, so the students who are interested in such activities are asked to stay back in school after the school hours (not possible for many students as transport back home becomes a problem). This reduces the number of students taking part and gives the school an excuse that they announce the activities but the students are not interested and do not take part. The schools must do these activities during the school timings and encourage a maximum number of students to participate.

Monitoring system to ensure teachers and schools are

following the set norms

Monitoring the teachers is done by the school authorities properly as they are required to fillup forms to be submitted to the Education Department. They keep the teachers under pressure of losing their jobs. The monitoring of teachers and schools by Education Inspectors is a thing of the past. Earlier, Education Inspectors used to visit schools, go through all the registers and files, talk to the teachers and ask them questions about their methods of teaching etc. These Education Inspectors also used to come to the classes and ask the students questions and check their understanding. The visit of the Education Inspector used to be once in a year and schools used to do all the efforts to showcase that they were following all the norms. While doing the white wash and cosmetic changes, they were forced to adhere to at least 80% of the norms to get an okay from the Education Inspectors.

Now-a-days, Education Inspectors do not visit the schools at all, and if at all they visit, they do 3-4 schools in one day, reducing it to only a 'Hi/hello' visit where they come face to face with the school authorities and have tea/coffee and nothing more. Many Education Inspectors call school authorities to their office with records where school authorities can conveniently forget to carry some records and apologize promptly. This leads to a higher level of opportunities for corruption and blatantly not following the set norms. All this has to stop, and we must ensure that the student to teacher ratio improves. All the students should get all the facilities. Schools should not OVERCHARGE and parents should be willing to pay reasonable fees. We have to think about the future of our country which rests in the hands of these students in secondary schools who are going to be citizens of tomorrow.

Points that bear repetition in order to stay with us:

i. Schools should be free to charge any amount of fee but should be taxed if they are making profits beyond a fixed limit.

ii. Parents should choose schools that they can afford and should not fight with schools over the fee structure.

iii. Municipal schools should be available in every ward and those who cannot afford private schools, should send their wards to municipal schools and fight with the civic authorities for good facilities.

iv. No examination till the Eighth standard is simply foolishness, and if students are unable to pass the exams, penalize the teachers and ask them to improve their teaching.

v. Objective questions should be only be used sparingly and there should be more of explanatory, descriptive and application based questions.

vi. Physical education and hobby classes should be made compulsory.

vii. Participation in inter-school tournaments for various subjects like elocution, quiz and various sports must be made compulsory for all schools.

viii. Junk food and soft drinks should be banned in the school premises.

ix. Compulsory physical fitness should be undertaken for each student and parents should be counselled if the child is not physically fit.

x. Parent-teacher meetings should be regularly held.

xi. The quality of teachers should be ensured to be good, with maximum number of teachers on a permanent basis.

xii. Students are found to be weak at verbal communication, so communication classes must be held in all the schools at all the levels to ensure proper diction and communication skills.

20. Education System - Higher Education

Higher education in India is normally defined as college education leading to a Bachelor's degree or education after the secondary school education leading to a Diploma certification. It talks about acquiring a degree or a diploma and not education. I have seen that most of the students applying for admission to the post graduate degree in management are unable to fill admission forms without outside help, unable to get a demand draft made, unable to introduce themselves and unable to answer simple general knowledge questions like what is the name of our Prime Minister or President They do not have any hobby but the answer as tutored by the tutorial classes is that they play some games or they like listening to music or reading novels. If you ask them to name any famous player in the game they are interested in, they are unable to answer. If you ask them what kind of music they like, they do not know that music can be classified into various types and mostly say film music but ask them any song of any particular music director and they are unable to relate a music director with any particular song. Ask them about the latest book they have read and they are unable to answer and if they talk about any book they know, they do not know the author of the book. What is the use of these graduates who cannot think on their own, do not know how to open an account in a bank, or travel to another part of the city unescorted? Will you call these people as highly educated? They are like pupils of primary schools. But look at their confidence; they think they have conquered Mt. Everest. The reason behind their confidence is that -

1. They have the latest mobile/tab.

2. They wear fashionable clothes of international brands.

3. They have a motorcycle/scooter of the latest type.

4. They have money in their pocket which they can spend on a girlfriend or have a boyfriend who spends on them.

5. They smoke and party.

None of these things that they are proud of have been earned by them; everything has been provided by their parents. Ask them, "What is YOUR ACHIEVEMENT in all this?" They do not have any answer.

Most people think that degrees get them jobs but they do not understand the difference between a degree and a qualifying degree as a shortlisting criteria. A degree can get you shortlisted but cannot give you a job unless you impress upon the interviewer that you are qualified to be selected.

- Is it the fault of the students passing out of

universities with graduation certificate? OR

- Is it the fault of the teachers teaching them? OR

- Is it the fault of a system that is focusing on awarding the maximum number of degree certificates, that sacrifices the quality of education? OR

- Is it the fault of the overburdened universities which are unable to cope up with the workload? OR

- Is it the collective responsibility of all the stakeholders?

If we start looking at the reasons, one by one, we find the following:

Fault of the students: When we start looking at the student's responsibility in the downgrading of education we find the following points:

1. They want a degree from age old universities, so they oppose the splitting of existing universities into new universities.

2. They want objective oriented examinations where they are not required to write and explain any concepts with examples (descriptive questions not required).

3. They want to get 100 out of 100 in all the subjects as a top score even in subjects like languages and social sciences.

4. The question papers must be theoretical and not

application based or else the student unions will agitate and declare the questions as out of syllabus.

5. The question papers must have questions of a repetitive type and easy to pass for all the students. If more than 20% students fail in any examination, the student's union will agitate and force the university to take re-examination or promote the students.

6. Students found copying repetitively also cannot be debarred from the examination. He/she must be allowed to appear for the remaining examination.

7. Students failing in 80% of the subjects also should be allowed to keep term.

8. Question papers and assessment system for backlog examination should be such that most of the students will be able to clear it.

9. The institute must give full marks to all students in internal examinations even if the student has not attended the classes and has still appeared for internal examinations.

10. Institutes cannot enforce any type of discipline on the students. They can enter the classes at will, keep messaging in the class, and sleep in the class etc.

No one wants to face student agitations as that can lead to students' complaints to the university authorities on real and concocted issues.

Fault of teachers: Teachers are also equally responsible for the current condition of higher education. Most of the teachers do not give importance to updating their knowledge of their subject and making it interesting for the students. We can list their defects as follows:

1. Not updating subject knowledge.

2. Not relating the subject to its practical use in reality.

3. Not giving practical examples in the Indian context.

4. Not suggesting changes in the syllabus like additions of newer, relevant topics and deletion of outdated topics.

5. Not willing to help students in solving their subjectrelated problems.

6. Unable to answer subject queries raised by the students instantly and without referring to the book.

7. Not coming to class in time.

8. Allowing students to come late for the class'

9. Not objecting to students' misbehavior in the class.

10. Not trying to create the teacher student bond and win respect of the students.

Because of these problems, students do not respect the teachers and unless made compulsory, do not attend the classes of such teachers. Comments like the following are very common in all colleges:

"He/she only tells us that it is available in so and so book, so why not read the book instead of attending the class?"

"You ask him/her one difficulty and he/she calls you after two days so that he/she can get it solved from other teachers and then explain it to us."

"He/she will only come to the class when more than 40 students are present. This can never happen for his/her class and so he/she declares the subject completed without taking the class." In Europe and USA, the student to teacher ratio is as low as 3:1 and a maximum of 15:1. What then, is the Indian ratio? 100:1or more... How do we expect good quality teaching with such a high load? Unless we increase the number of colleges and universities where the student to teacher ratio is brought down to around 30:1, we cannot expect better quality education and that students passing out of colleges will become worthy of good jobs, without much of training. Many teachers are interested in university politics and try and get posted on various committees in the University and remain absent from the college citing the attendance of various meetings. Appointment on the various committees is a source of earning additional income when they go for inspections of various colleges.

Fault of the system focusing on awarding the maximum number of degree certificates: Nobody forces anyone to award degree certificates to the maximum number of students. It is an excuse created by the college administration and teachers to hide their lacuna in the quality of their teaching. All the colleges are interested in attracting the maximum number of student enrollments (not attendance). More student enrolments mean that the college has a better standing. To maintain their standing among students, the college must ensure that the quality of teaching is good and if that is not possible they should try and ensure that quality of question papers is bad (thus all can pass). This is the harsh reality. These colleges even encourage mass copying at the time of examinations. Since a maximum numbers of colleges are doing the same, it enters into the educational system. Serious students interested in getting quality education try and enroll themselves in colleges where the quality of teaching is good and we see some colleges having an admission cut-off percentage of 90% in the qualifying (HSC) examinations.

Fault of the overburdened Universities: Universities are overburdened with workload as most of the Universities cater to more than 400 colleges under them when ideally every University must only cater to a maximum of 60-75 colleges. The following table shows the number of colleges under various universities in India.

Sr.No.	Name of University	Arts & Commerce,	Science, Computer Sc.	Engg.	Arch.	Pharma	Mgmt.	Law	Education	Total
1	Mumbai	82	169	92	15	20	63	31	68	540
2	Pune SPPU	294		61	11	47	168	24	110	705
3	Aurangabad BAMU	Details not available on website								423
4	Shivaji	177		35	3	15	Included in arts & commerce	7	42	279
5	Solapur	Details not available on website								119
6	North Maharashtra	118		21		10	40	8	43	240
7	Amravati SGBAU	Details not available on website								
8	Nagpur RTMNU	139								
9	Nanded SRTM	Details not available on website								415

It can be seen that only Solapur University which takes care of only one district has 119 colleges and the maximum number of colleges affiliated to any university in Maharashtra is Pune University. Ironically, Pune University has the maximum number of problems about conducting examinations and declaration of results. In this regards, Pune University, (now called Savitribai Phule Pune University) compares with Magadh University of Bodh Gaya in Bihar where results are declared after one or two years after conducting the examinations and still students keep protesting and ask for correction in the results.

Why we are not dividing universities into many parts and ensuring that every university has a maximum of 50-75 colleges under them? In Europe and USA, universities have a lesser number of colleges, better reputations and world rankings. The administrative staff can better monitor the progress of all the colleges and ensure that they all follow the required policy standards. All faculty members can then be in touch with each other and decide on updating of the syllabus easily and also agree to have examinations based on application-oriented questions where students will be able to apply the concepts they learn and will have a better knowledge of the subject. Comparison between the faculties will force them to update their knowledge and also go in for further research. This will further improve the quality of teaching and the reputation of the universities. The Government will not have any additional burden as the number of students would remain the same and so the student welfare expenses would also remain the same. The only change that may happen is that the universities will use the entire grant that the Government gives them for development (presently it remains unused).

USA, with 1/10th the population of India has 4000+ universities whereas, India has only 422 universities. This must change. We need to have at least 4000, if not 40000 universities. Let us allow universities having only one college under them but having world ranking under 100.

Collective responsibility of all the stakeholders:

From all the above discussions, we will find that the responsibility is not collective. Students would be forced to take admissions as per their marks in the qualifying examinations. The universities with a high reputation will have higher cut-off percentages for admissions and universities with low reputation will have lower cut-offs. Students will be willing to pay more fees for better universities, thus increasing the university/college collection. So they will pay a better salary to their faculty, thus attracting better and better faculty. The responsibility rests squarely on the Government and teachers who are not allowing the break-up of the universities (Maharashtra had only one university - University of Mumbai, and then added one more University of Nagpur when the state was formed. Now it has nine state universities and many private universities. Why not have 100 universities?)

Points to ponder

1. Allow private universities to open colleges, and allow them to charge fees on the open market principle. Good education should be expensive, let students choose which university/college they want to enter.

2. Professional colleges should have faculty with good working experience in the industry. (One institute had an Assistant Professor in Marketing having two years [24 months] of work experience in six companies, averaging four months per

company i.e. he was never confirmed in any company).

3. Salaries of professors should have no upper limit, a professor with useful research projects and consultancy should be paid more than the others.

4. Good teachers will ensure good attendance and also ensure that attendance marks are not given without having physical attendance in the class.

5. Continuous evaluation should be based on applied original projects and the faculty should decide the marks.

6. The syllabus should be broad-based and not specific and the faculty should be allowed to decide pedagogy.

7. Students should not be allowed to have agitations against passing percentages and out-of-syllabus questions.

8. Government Universities should have a maximum of 100 colleges under them.

9. The NAC should decide the fee structure of colleges based on the infrastructure, quality of faculty, quality of syllabus, examination patterns, quality of question papers (percentage of application-based questions), students' feedback and students' employability.

10. The NAC certification should be initially valid only for three years and subsequently for five years.

21. Educational System - Professional Education

When we talk of professional education it can be classified into certificate courses, diploma courses, degree courses and post-graduate courses. We need to talk about all these courses separately and differently as all these courses have a different level of input from the faculty and the students have a different level of capacity for output.

Certificate courses: We in India have various certificate courses in professional education like the following:

1. Computer related courses:

i. CCNA

ii. Software testing

iii. Technical writing

iv. SAP/other ERP courses

v. JAVA/J2EEE

vi. Photoshop

vii.DTP

    viii. Accountancy modules

     ix. Hardware maintenance and installations

2. **Skills development courses:**

    i.   Secretarial course (steno/typist)

    ii.   Office administration and filing

    iii. Electrician

    iv. Plumbing

    v.   Draftsman

    vi. Machine operators

       a. Turners

       b. Fitters

       c. Cutters, punch machine operators

    vii. Mason

    viii. Welders

    ix. Carpenter

    x.   Furniture polishing

    xi. Automobile mechanics

    xii. General mechanics

    xiii. Selling & salesmanship

    xiv. Telephone operator

    xv. Tele-callers (BPO)

    xvi. Eye testing/spectaclemaking

xvii. Radio/TV/Computer repairs

Eligibility for most of these courses is SSC pass and even school drop-outs can join these programs and get the certifications. All these courses are offered by Government-sponsored Industrial Training Institutes or privately run institutes like the Kohinoor Institute and Indo-American Society in Maharashtra. In those which are Government–run, the eligibility criteria are strict but privately-run institutes relax the eligibility on the basis of personal interviews. In some places, industries open up their own skill development institutes which ensure that the students joining these institutes are trained to operate particular machines and/or able to do specific jobs as required by that particular industry.

Fortunately, the input by all the faculties is very good and students passing out of these institutes are found to be able to do the required work efficiently. Many students are found investing in their own business enterprises.

More number of such institutes need to be opened in many parts of rural India so that skilled manpower to do such skilled jobs would be available all over India and people need not travel to major cities for getting this training. The people who get trained in cities never go back and work in rural India.

Diploma courses: Professional diploma courses are of four types:

1. Career enhancement courses.

2. Engineering diplomas.

3. Super-specialty diplomas in medicine.

4. Skills development diplomas.

Career enhancement diplomas: The trouble starts with this type of diploma courses as they are not job-oriented and getting a job on the basis of any diploma (unless it is specialized and rare) is difficult. Many people who are already working somewhere like to take diplomas as a career improvement instrument. Hence, they take up diplomas that are available as part-time courses or on distance learning mode. In this case, the student is interested in getting a certificate and not the inputs, as this certificate can help him/her get promoted in the current job. Institutes offering these types of diplomas are also aware of this reality and tell the students that they would grant them leave of absence and give them full internal marks and allow them to appear for the final examination. Many institutes even approach various industries and canvass with their personnel departments to send their students for such courses and offer to give crash lessons on weekends so that these people are not required to attend classes in the institute and still get a broad idea of the subject. In this case, everyone is aware that the inputs are only theoretical and serve no practical purpose and that the students are doing these courses to cross the stipulated hurdle of the management degree. Most universities ask repetitive questions so that students can be well-prepared to answer them and get better scores. Even the assessment is not done very strictly.

The distance learning formats are more student-friendly

where the students are required to do assignments and appear for one examination in a year. The assignments are mostly copied from study materials and are accepted without questioning as assessment is rarely done. The yearly examination is on the basis of important/likely questions given in the study materials. Students are likely to fail once or twice in subjects where numerical ability based questions are asked, but they barely clear by getting passing marks in the third attempt.

Engineering diplomas: When students take a full-time diploma course like engineering diplomas, they try to get a high rank in their final year so that they can enter engineering degree colleges for a degree course on the basis of their scores in the final examination. In such cases, students are serious about their studies and teachers are trying to prove themselves by ensuring that the maximum students get better scores in their subjects.

Many students are found taking admission to diploma on the basis of their SSC marks after they are unable to get admission to the engineering course on the basis of their HSC marks. This trend has stopped as admission to engineering courses has become easy with thousands of engineering seats going vacant. Also, getting bank loans for engineering degree courses is also becoming easier, the demand for engineering diplomas is going down and in due course of time, many institutes will stop running these courses.

Super-specialty diplomas in medicine: With the importance of a degree in medicine and the quality of education in medicine going down and the fees going up, all people want to be treated by specialists only. The General Practitioners do not like to do house calls and so patients are forced to get admitted to nursing homes. While getting admitted, their choice is to get admitted to the best of the nursing homes run by doctors with super-specialty diplomas after doing their masters in medicine or surgery. So, patients having no serious ailments also get admitted to various nursing homes. With many people covered under medical insurance either by their employers or on their own, there are no financial restrictions and so they choose the best (doctors having many degrees are supposed to be good).

In this case, the quality of education becomes immaterial and the focus is on the doctor's experience and his not having a blot on his career.

Degree courses: We have various professional degree courses that can be classified into various sub-heads to find the quality that is being dished out to the students:

1. Engineering & technical courses: Various engineering and technical courses are offered by Indian universities. Some of them give very specialized knowledge and some of them give general engineering or technical knowledge with a new subject thrown in and called 'specialization' to attract students. We will look into them separately.

    a) Engineering courses: Engineering courses with various specializations are being offered by all the universities ranging from basic electrical, mechanical and civil streams to chemical, textile and aeronautical engineering. Students prefer computer, electronics and tele-communications as they lead to instant high-paying jobs. No one is interested in engineering jobs that make them work in production. Even students passing out of mechanical engineering prefer sales and marketing jobs and are not interested in working on the shop floor. This shows that an engineering education is preferred for better paying jobs rather than interest in the engineering field. So we may find that many engineers passing out of IITs (premier technology institutes set up by the Government of India - i.e. Indian Institutes of Technology) with space technology as specialization, join IIMs (Indian Institutes of Management), do a course in marketing and end up selling, may-be match boxes! The reason is that they are looking for well-paying jobs.

The engineering institutes do not generate enough interest in their students to work in the manufacturing field, use their knowledge for inventing newer methods of manufacturing with cost reduction and improved quality of products, and develop newer products of world standards.

Korea was well-known for manufacturing and selling duplicates of all kinds of products in 1970s and was strife-torn. Today their products are leading the charts all over the world because of an engineering revolution (Samsung, Hyundai, LG), because their engineers developed newer and newer products with lower and lower costs of production and better and better quality.

Indian engineers are unable to give us basic facilities like stable electric load, plain roads, dependable buildings, bridges etc. We are required to look West or East for newer technology and one can easily say that any Government department with a higher number of engineer employees is inefficient in their work e.g. PWD, Electricity Boards, and Telecom departments.

Why are we not able to produce world class engineers who can produce world class products indigenously, is a big question in everyone's mind.

b) **Technical courses:** Various technical courses are available in India that can be listed as follows:

- Rubber technology

- Leather technology

- Plastics technology

Most of these institutes offering specialized courses are run by the Government of India as the number of students joining them are less so they are commercially not viable for private players. All the technological subjects having more students interested in joining are being run by various engineering degree colleges. Since the intake is very small (annually 30 students), these institutes maintain a high quality of input and output.

2. Management courses: Many universities offer degree courses in management like BBA (Bachelor in Business Administration), and BMS (Bachelor in

Management Science). While we can say that this course gives a detailed outline of the business environment, it lacks in many ways to qualify the students for any particular job and so all of them either end up doing the job of sales persons in retail stores or other organizations. Students with this degree have an option to join the post-graduate courses in management for enhancing their chances of getting jobs. Students with management degrees find it easy to clear all the first year subjects in post-graduate (MBA) courses as many universities do not offer better syllabus than the final year BBA/BMS courses.

It would be a good idea if these BBA/BMS graduates who have secured distinction in their third year, with at least first class in the first two years and have done good projects should be allowed to take admission to the second year MBA course (specialization to be decided on the basis of the project and third year marks).

3. Medical courses: We have various medical courses such as MBBS (Allopathic), BAMS (Ayurveda), BHMS (Homeopathic), BUMS (Unani) and B. Pharmacy. All these courses churn out graduates with different quality of expertise. Students of pharmacy education get jobs instantly as pharmacists in medical retail shops (it is compulsory to have a pharmacist all day long in each and every medicine shop) or can start their own medicine shop. They also get recruited in various pathology laboratories as chemists. The

MBBS graduates try for further education, through post-graduation, getting specialization and super specialization as they do not have the confidence of starting their own dispensary (now called clinic) and earning a decent livelihood (competition is high in cities and no one wants to go to towns and villages).

How do we instil the confidence of private practice in these MBBS graduates? How can we make these MBBS graduates open their clinics in towns and villages? What will make them feel safe and secure without getting specialization and super specialization degrees and earn a decent livelihood?

The graduates with all the other degrees start their clinics and dispense allopathic medicines, as most of the patients are interested in quick relief (The Government is even thinking of allowing them to do allopathic practice by giving them a short course in pharmacology). Why did they study Ayurveda or Homeopathy in the first place? Because they were unable to get admission to the MBBS course!

4.   Media and publication courses: With increase in media companies with publication and broadcasting on various TV channels, radio stations and so many newspapers and magazines, the demand for media personnel has gone up. Along with it many private institutes are coming out with various degree and diploma courses in media and publications.

There are many media houses which run their own

media training programmes, giving degrees and diplomas with job guarantee in the same media house. The idea is very simple; the media house gets trainees who are paying a high amount of fees (instead of getting stipend) and then working for a few years as trainees with stipend. Media houses have their employee requirements fulfilled at a very low cost or no cost at all.

A major problem in this training and giving degrees is that it may train these people how to write or dispatch a column or train them in an acceptable communication level, but do not train them in general knowledge, history or geography of the region. This leads to major faux pas, as a reporter reporting in his dispatch wrote, "There was a major accident near Tirupathi in the state of Tamil Nadu----". This even gets printed in the newspapers as the editing is non-existent (there are only page–setters, who fit the dispatches received on e-mail without reading. Sometimes, they put the same news twice on different pages or even on the same page. Sometimes, one or two lines are omitted, leaving the readers guessing the full news). In most of the newspaper offices, no one reads the news. I had personal discussions with a senior editor of a leading newspaper when we went together to see the biscuit factory where I was the marketing head, about the spelling mistakes in newspapers from the media group where he worked. He said that the deadline pressure does not allow them to do proper editing and most of the time no one notices it also.

Now if this is the case of the world's largest selling newspaper, what can we expect from others? All the media personnel (people do not like to be called journalists as it limits them) should take courses in general knowledge, history and geography of the region where they are going to be active.

5. Law courses: Law courses give a degree in law called LLB. Having this degree you become competent to start private practice or become an assistant to a successful lawyer where you can do apprenticeship for some time and later start your own practice. Like any other profession, you need to establish yourself as a good lawyer before clients start flocking to your office.

    Many law graduates join various other organizations as legal advisors, for example, in banks or in Human Resource Departments where the knowledge of legal proceedings is essential while doing day-to-day work.

    After some years of legal practice, one can even appear for competitive examinations and become a magistrate of the lower courts, where one can later rise to become a judge. The legal degree that is being given is good enough to become a professional in the legal field.

6. Foreign language courses: With globalization, foreign language courses are gaining importance. One can join various organizations doing business with foreign organizations for understanding and doing correspondence with them. Multinational

companies and banks prefer such people for their operations. A foreign language degree holder can even start his/her own foreign language classes to teach that language to those who are interested in doing business with any such foreign country. They can also become free-lance interpreters for foreign delegates/tourists and earn a decent income.

7. Computer courses: Apart from engineering degrees in computers, there are other degrees in computers like B.Sc. (Computers), BCS (Bachelor of Computer Sciences), BCA (Bachelor of Computer Administration) which give the students enough knowledge to join software companies. All the computer graduates with good English communication skills and confidence are able to get good jobs that pay well and get a chance to go abroad.

8. Animation courses: Animation is a new field where there are numerous employment opportunities for creative persons. They can get employed by various advertising agencies, motion picture houses or they can be self-employed and work freelance for various companies. Many animation experts from India have done great jobs for Hollywood production houses.

People who do not have a creative ability or who are not artists should not venture into this field, as they do not have any scope here. Many Animation Technology Institutes started (mushroomed is the right word maybe) some years ago, enrolled students who had no creative abilities, either in drawings or in languages and they could not get any jobs and so the enrolments stopped and the institutes shut down. One should not make it a money-making racket as it cannot be sustained for long.

9. Designing courses: Designing courses are of two types.

Fashion designing: Plenty of institutes are offering courses in fashion designing at certificate and diploma levels and very few at the degree level. Many institutes that offer degree courses are offering degrees from foreign universities and not Indian universities. NIFT (National Institute of Fashion Technology) is sponsored by the Union Ministry of Textile, Government of India. They have many campuses across India and give quality education in fashion and knowledge in textiles which is very important for a fashion designer.

Any person who is seriously interested in a career in fashion designing should do a degree course in fashion designing from NIFT. They can further do post graduate course also in the same field through NIFT.

Industrial designing: Industrial designing is gaining momentum in India with many industrial houses trying to come out with their own products in various categories that need to be elegant-looking, cost-effective (use of light weight but strong materials that are cost-effective) and easy to produce and maintain. The Indian Automobile sector is leading in this field and they want aerodynamic designs that are aesthetically good- looking and consume lesser fuel (high fuel efficiency). Companies like Mahindra & Mahindra have come out with many indigenous models that have worldwide acceptance as sturdy and fuel-efficient vehicles.

The Government of India has established three national institutes of design at Ahmedabad, Delhi and Bengaluru, as they want quality design engineers who can help in developing Indian products in Defence and other industrial sectors like aviation, shipping and other fields. The number of seats in all these institutes is very limited and only students with a high calibre in designing can get through them.

Many private institutes have also opened up, giving courses in industrial designing and some of them offer degrees of foreign universities to their students. This field is still not very popular and so they are still maintaining quality standards.

10. Fine Art Courses: Many Fine Art institutes in India offer diploma courses in the following fields:

   a. Indoor & Outdoor Drawing and sketching

   b. Geometrical Drawing & Perspective Drawing

   c. Drawing (Full Figure)

   d. Portrait

   e. Nature study

   f. Still-life composition

   g. Pictorial composition

   h. Portrait painting

   i. Art & aesthetics

   j. Colour study

   k. History of Indian Art

   l. Painting - all mediums

  m. Material & methods

   n. Aesthetics

   o. Clay Modelling

   p. Calligraphy

   q. Visual communication

   r. Art direction

   s. Advertising

   t. Web designing

   u. Photography

   v. Copy-writing

  w. Graphic design

The only recognized degree course in Fine Arts is offered by MS University, Vadodara which was established with the blessings of Maharaja Sayajirao Gaikwad of erstwhile Baroda state. In the University of Mumbai, JJ School of Arts offers a degree course in arts like sculpture, modelling, ceramics, metal works, architecture, interior design but it cannot be termed as specialized in Fine Art courses.

The quality of education in this field depends on the teachers and so, one must check the reputation of the institute before joining it.

Post-graduate degrees: Very few institutes were offering post-graduate degrees earlier, as the degree itself was considered high quality education and was enough to get best the jobs. But as the number of institutes are growing and professional education has become mass--based, the quality standards have dropped and students passing out with certificate, diploma and degree courses are no longer assured of good jobs. Another aspect of professional education are the AICTE (All India Council for Technical Education) norms of minimum 'first-class post graduate degree' for all the teachers in professional institutes. This is leading people who are inclined to become teachers (professors) in professional education, to seek admission to post graduate courses. Many institutes are starting post graduate courses to create availability of fresh teachers who comply with AICTE norms.

Since these institutes are trying to create a pool of teachers with first class post graduate degree, the quality of the post graduate course had dropped.

Summary:

To summarize professional education, one can very well say that wherever education is limited to a small number of students and institutes, the quality of education is good and wherever it has become mass-based and commercial (churning out the maximum number of students for making the institute commercially viable), the quality standards have fallen and can be termed as low level education.

The need for establishing more number of universities without any limit on the fee structure and having market operated admissions is urgent. Let the students choose the best institute/university where he pays more to get quality education that ensures good employment. These universities can offer scholarships to deserving candidates to ensure a good input of quality students.

www.ingramcontent.com/pod-product-compliance
Lightning Source LLC
Chambersburg PA
CBHW030546030726
47495CB00004B/1155